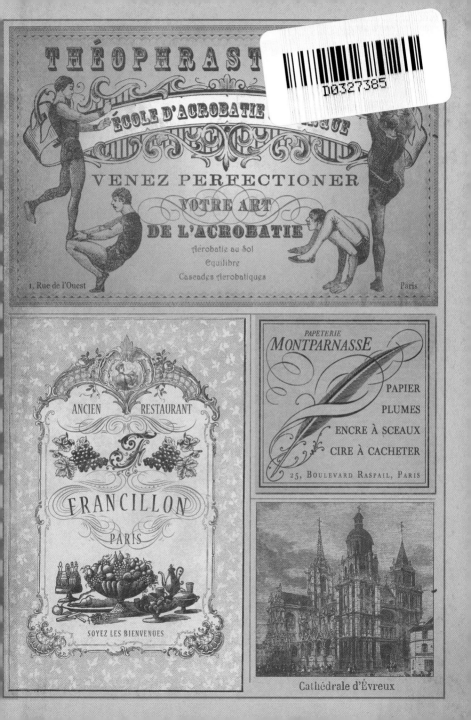

THÉOPHRASTE

ÉCOLE D'ACROBATIE *[...]*QUE

VENEZ PERFECTIONER
VOTRE ART
DE L'ACROBATIE

Acrobatie au Sol
Equilibre
Cascades Acrobatiques

1, Rue de l'Ouest   Paris

ANCIEN   RESTAURANT

FRANCILLON
PARIS

SOYEZ LES BIENVENUES

PAPETERIE
MONTPARNASSE

PAPIER
PLUMES
ENCRE À SCEAUX
CIRE À CACHETER

25, BOULEVARD RASPAIL, PARIS

Cathédrale d'Évreux

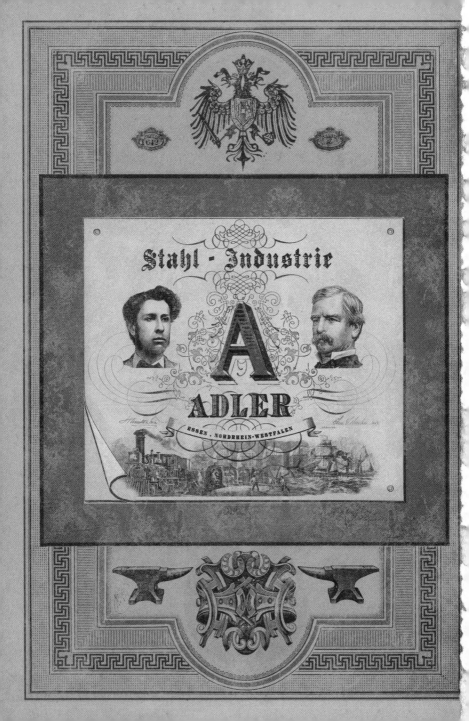

Sherlock, Lupin & Me is published by Capstone Young Readers
A Capstone Imprint
1710 Roe Crest Drive
North Mankato, Minnesota 56003
www.capstoneyoungreaders.com

© 2013 Atlantyca Dreamfarm s.r.l., Italy
© 2016 for this book in English language – (Stone Arch Books/Capstone Young Readers)
Text by Pierdomenico Baccalario and Alessandro Gatti
Editorial project by Atlantyca Dreamfarm S.r.l., Italy
Translated into the English language by Nanette McGuinness
Original edition published by Edizioni Piemme S.p.A., Italy
Original title: La cattedrale della paura

International Rights © Atlantyca S.p.A., via Leopardi 8 - 20123 Milano – Italia – foreignrights@atlantyca.it – www.atlantyca.com
No part of this book may be stored, reproduced or transmitted in any form or by any means, electronic or mechanical, including photocopying, recording, or by any information storage and retrieval system, without written permission from the copyright holder. For information address Atlantyca S.p.A.

Library of Congress Cataloging-in-Publication Data
Adler, Irene (Fictitious character), author.
 [Cattedrale della paura. English]

 The cathedral of fear / by Irene Adler ; illustrated by Iacopo Bruno ; text by Pierdomenico Baccalario and Alessandro Gatti.

     pages cm. -- (Sherlock, Lupin & me)
 Translation of: La Cattedrale della paura.

 Summary: In March 1871 Irene's family moves from London to Evreux in Normandy, but after a strange woman warns her that her mother is in danger, Irene calls upon her friends Arsène Lupin and Sherlock Holmes for help and soon the three young detectives are caught up in the search for an ancient relic said to be in a secret crypt beneath the streets of Paris — a Paris which is torn apart by war and currently ruled by the Commune.

 ISBN 978-1-4965-0490-6 (library binding)
 ISBN 978-1-62370-257-1 (paper over board)
 ISBN 978-1-4965-0491-3 (pbk.)
 ISBN 978-1-62370-573-2 (ebook)
 ISBN 978-1-4965-2348-8 (ebook pdf)

 1. Adler, Irene (Fictitious character)--Juvenile fiction. 2. Holmes, Sherlock--Juvenile fiction. 3. Lupin, Arsène (Fictitious character)--Juvenile fiction. 4. Relics--Juvenile fiction. 5. Detective and mystery stories. 6. Paris (France)--History--Commune, 1871--Juvenile fiction. 7. Evreux (France)--History--19th century--Juvenile fiction. [1. Mystery and detective stories. 2. Characters in literature--Fiction. 3. Paris (France)--History--Commune, 1871--Fiction. 4. Evreux (France)--History--19th century--Fiction. 5. France--History--19th century--Fiction.] I. Bruno, Iacopo, illustrator. II. Baccalario, Pierdomenico, author. III. Gatti, Alessandro, 1975- author. IV. Title.

 PZ7.A261545Cat 2016
 [Fic]--dc23
                        2015004543

Designer: Peggie Carley

Printed in China.
03312015   008866RRDF15

IRENE ADLER

SHERLOCK, LUPIN & ME

THE CATHEDRAL OF FEAR

by Irene Adler

Illustrations by Jacopo Bruno

capstone
young readers

TABLE OF CONTENTS

Chapter 1
RETURNING HOME.. 7

Chapter 2
A COUNTRY VILLAGE 17

Chapter 3
A LILAC-COLORED ROOM 25

Chapter 4
GRACEFUL HANDWRITING.....................................39

Chapter 5
AN UNEXPECTED GUEST 51

Chapter 6
THE RIVER..63

Chapter 7
REVISIONS..73

Chapter 8
SNAPS AND SECRETS.. 87

Chapter 9
A GOOD REPAIR 97

Chapter 10
THE MONTMORENCYS..107

Chapter 11
A JOINT DECISION...125

Chapter 12
THE ALCHEMISTS OF PARIS 135

Chapter 13
THE DUMAS ARCHIVES 147

Chapter 14
THE LADY OF THE CAMELLIAS 155

Chapter 15
THE CARDINAL'S CAVERN 171

Chapter 16
DESCENT INTO DARKNESS.......................................183

Chapter 17
THE DARK HEART OF PARIS 193

Chapter 18
THE MASTER'S VOICE 201

Chapter 19
AN EMPEROR 215

Chapter 20
THE DARKEST TRUTH 225

Chapter 21
AN EXTRAORDINARY DAY 239

Chapter 1

RETURNING HOME

Wars are never fought only in the field. Especially when looked at from a distance with the knowing eyes of an adult — eyes that confuse black smoke fires with the glow of bonfires, in order to reassure children. As we passed through the French countryside during the slow stages of our return trip across the continent, protected by the gentle hills and the dense layers of trees, we could imagine that everything we had heard in the announcements on the radio was false. But that was not the case, and we all knew it. We had fled far away, Papa, Mama, and I. But now we were returning.

Newspaper boys who couldn't themselves read fanned the darkened pages of the papers loudly, and the names that I heard — *Le Mans, Saint-Quentin, Lisaine* — flew through my head like swallows. I had chosen to take in nothing about the war, because I knew that if I merely began to ask about what was happening to my city — to Paris — I might go crazy with grief. Or, even worse, I would ask to go back to the home we had left six months before.

Actually, an entire winter had passed since we took the ferry from Calais to Dover. From there we had gone to London on one of those amazing trains that the English were famous for. According to my father, the ferry on the outbound trip would signal the beginning of our new life. A drastic break — like the stroke of a knife — between what had taken place before and what would happen there, in England, far from the war that kept disturbing Paris.

During the months we had spent across the English Channel in London, the French had lost all they could lose — a war and much of their dignity. Again, this was according to my father, who was not actually French, although he had always lived in Paris. He was Prussian, like the victors of the war, and this put him in a strange light in the eyes of all those who had been his friends. His major business contacts, too, although even during the war, this had not kept him from working. My father worked in the iron business. And while he never admitted to me that iron from the Adler steelworks was used to produce muskets and cannonballs, I did think that from a certain point of view, Papa had not minded the war so much.

"Now is a time of great turmoil," he used to say to me when I was little, ruffling my hair. "Who knows if a better world will arise from it than the one we live in, my daughter?"

And with these words, "my daughter," I felt Papa's hand shake slightly — so slightly that it took me many years and adventures before I remembered that detail — a detail that's meaning is crystal clear to me now as I write.

"My daughter," my father used to say, before the war broke out and changed everything. The rich became poor, and rebels became statesmen. Soldiers became deserters, and deserters pretended to have fought to defend our flag. A flag that had been overwhelmed by the tumultuous events of those months, I discovered, much like so many other things.

"It seems as though France's flag no longer exists," Papa said one day during our return trip, reading the news. The flag was that of the Revolution: blue, white, and red.

"No? Well, what have they done with it?" my mother asked, shut into the safest corner of the carriage, her voice faint.

My father did not answer her, or if he did I did not hear, because I was studying the countryside gently rolling outside my window.

Another stroke of the knife, I was thinking — crossing the English Channel a second time, but this time in reverse, from Dover to Calais.

And London, smoky London, had disappeared into the gray.

★ ★ ★

Our return trip was not pleasant. And not just due to the condition of my mother's health.

I kept remembering how badly Mr. Horatio Nelson had suffered on the ferry after we'd left France the previous autumn. Later on, our family butler told me about a nasty experience he'd had many years before onboard a ship. When he was serving as an ordinary seaman, he was accused of having murdered a passenger and throwing her into the sea. Then, when the ship had landed in London, Scotland Yard had arrested him unjustly.

Now, during our return crossing from England to France, Mr. Nelson stood on the main deck, sniffing the air. Like a huge statue, he stood immobile, his gaze set toward the south, as if that way he could catch a glimpse of the glint of steel and the gunpowder exploding in the salty haze.

My father stayed in the cabin the whole time, watching over Mama. Pale as a tallow candle, she had disappeared into her bed, greatly weakened by consumption. The British doctors — and even the one whom my father had brought in from Vienna — were sure of the illness she was suffering from.

"A serious lung infection," they had said.

And that was that.

My father had looked at me with that deeply sympathetic expression I had already seen on his face at other times. Seeing it then again was the real reason I had not asked him if he had ever manufactured weapons, as well as train tracks and wheels.

"If even the Austrian doctor said so, my daughter, it must be true," he had whispered to me.

Papa had hoped to the bitter end that this was not the case. That my mother just had pneumonia or a particularly severe case of the flu, but nothing more. He comforted her, saying that spring would be coming soon, that this horrible London winter would be lifted by the blossoming cherry trees and the linden tree pollen in Hyde Park. But it did little good.

My mother's hands had grown increasingly pale, her pained bouts of coughing more pronounced, and her faint, scarce pulse ever weaker.

Tentacles of silence had spread through our Aldford Street apartment, broken only by the ticking of the pendulum and the clash of the Limoges dishes as Papa and I dined, barely exchanging a word.

"Do you still see your friend?" he'd asked me almost every evening, forgetting that my reply was always the same.

My friend was Sherlock Holmes, and yes, I had seen him regularly until my mother's sudden illness, which had reduced the frequency of our meetings.

"Are you still quite fond of each other?" Papa had asked.

Yes, we were. But something much more complicated was hidden beneath my father's question. Papa was thinking of moving again, of leaving London. And in that awkward way only men can do, he was trying to figure out how much the news would upset me.

Leaving London when we had scarcely arrived. It would not have upset me, if Papa had only asked me directly.

But he never did.

He only told me the date we would be leaving — just as the linden tree pollen would arrive, but without waiting for spring.

So we were returning to France, but not to Paris, because news from the capital didn't sound at all reassuring. Papa revealed the existence of a country estate in the town of Evreux, about a hundred kilometers west of Paris. It was there that we were headed in our carriage. And it was the hills of Evreux that I was examining out my window.

I pressed my knees between my hands, as if I had taken hold of something firm — a thought, an idea, or a sense of gloom. I forced myself to look at neither my father, his face as dark as a stormy sky, nor my mother across from him, pale as a ghost.

How had my mother's lungs become damaged like this? I wondered.

During one of the breaks on the long return trip, I asked Mr. Nelson what he knew about my mother's illness. Our butler simply shook his head.

"It's not what you think, Miss Irene," Mr. Nelson explained to me. "Your mother's illness is due to the city air. The chimney stacks and the unhealthy smog from the factories that fill London. Your mother has very delicate lungs, and that air is like poison for her."

Indeed, it was true. There were days when it seemed there was a screen of suspended dust — of dense, suffocating soot. I remembered how the sudden rain pelting down had covered my clothes with rivulets like dark tears. My mother suffered badly from this, and it was only aggravated by her severe homesickness for France and French ways.

"Is that why we didn't go to live in the English countryside, somewhere like Bath or Oxford?" I asked Mr. Nelson.

I knew I should ask my father, but talking to him had become difficult. The happy, gentle man of a few months earlier — who had hugged me and spun me around in pirouettes — had hidden his feelings behind a closed curtain without warning, like a theater that had suddenly shut down.

"Your father thought returning to France would do your mother more good than any other cure," Mr. Nelson replied. "And I believe he was right."

I believed so, too, despite the chaos unfolding in our home country.

And so, on March 6, 1871, we returned.

Chapter 2

A COUNTRY VILLAGE

The country home my father had bought was just outside the village of Evreux, a town of squat, little houses tightly surrounding a majestic cathedral that frightened me when I glimpsed it from the carriage. It was visible from far away, and with its double bell tower and pointed spires like the tips of arrows, it soared above the other buildings in the village. The central rose window facing the park looked like a whirlwind to me. I turned away.

"There are your cathedrals." My father smiled, gently patting my mother's hand. "Do you feel a bit more at home now, my dear?"

17

Mama nodded, and a weak smile lit her face.

A flock of crows disturbed our passage as we left the cathedral and the village shops behind us and rode over the arched bridge.

Our new home suddenly appeared on the left, but I could not see it clearly from where I sat in the carriage. It was too much for me to stand.

"Irene!" Papa shouted when he saw me fumbling with the lock on the carriage door.

I didn't hear anything past that. I opened the door wide and leaned out, clinging to the brass bar of the luggage rack that ran right above the window. With a single swift movement, I pulled myself up, just as Arsène Lupin, my other dear friend, had taught me.

Two pairs of stunned eyes stared at me from the coachman's box, but then Mr. Nelson signaled the driver to continue as if everything were normal.

"Be careful with the luggage, Miss Irene," he warned me in a tone of voice that, nonetheless, did not seem at all worried. "I'm not sure they were tied together well."

I sat down on one of my mother's trunks. Meanwhile, from inside the carriage, my father pounded the ceiling under my feet with the knob of his walking stick, trying to convince me to come back inside where a young lady like me belonged. It seemed as though my mother's illness had encouraged Papa to see things more from her perspective.

I snorted and concentrated on what I could see.

The house had an expansive garden descending all the way to the banks of a river, melting into a dense bed of reeds. I spied a wooden jetty stretching over the water. Then the carriage changed direction, turning onto the main road, which was flanked by two rows of centuries-old elm trees.

The house was as cute as a button. It had two stories and a third row of round windows peeping over the roof. The gate was covered with vines and had not been closed properly. The many branches that had fallen on the dirt road snapped noisily under the horses' hooves. Someone had arranged for the shutters to be opened before we arrived, but it was obvious that the house had been empty the previous season. A wisp of smoke rose from the chimney top, which reassured me, since the country air was still brisk despite the scent of spring.

I went back inside the carriage and sighed with relief, noting that the grim cathedral was no longer visible. We traveled along the road as it ran past the entire garden before it continued on to the other estates. Venturing into the dense shadows projected from the branches, we finally stopped in front of the entrance to the house, where two servants were waiting for us, along with four stretcher-bearers who would help my mother.

Papa got out to direct the operations and disappeared into the house, seeming to forget that he had just been scolding me. I was struck by how he did all he could for my mother and how he clearly felt lost without her help.

Through the thick windowpanes, I watched the shadows of other people move inside the house for several minutes. Then I saw Mr. Nelson pass by, weighed down with luggage.

"What would you say if I gave you a hand?" I asked, taking advantage of my parents' absence to take a few liberties unthinkable for a young lady.

Without waiting for Mr. Nelson's reply — which I knew would be negative — I untied the ropes fastening the luggage. When he came back for a second trip, I unloaded the suitcases from the carriage, placing them in his arms.

At my back, the reeds along the riverbank gently swayed.

I did not go into the house right away. I walked along outside it, inspecting it with the careful eye of someone who has moved before, and would prefer to focus on what is wrong, rather than notice its delightful details.

Yet, despite my suspicions, I liked the house a great deal. And when I finished my tour, I saw something that chased away my last doubts.

I ran across the grass toward the riverbank, where a swing swayed from a tree near the water.

I could not believe how beautiful it was. I played with the ropes and the little wooden seat, feeling as if I were inside one of those bucolic scenes that the good society ladies loved to hang on the walls of their proper parlors. I shook my head at that thought, quickly giving in to the rocking of the swing.

I had to write to my friends right away. To let them know I was here and that they absolutely had to send me their news and come see . . .

I burst out laughing. What did they have to come see? A swing? A picturesque garden?

I waited until evening fell for someone to remember me.

Then, as soon as I heard someone calling my name, I went into the house.

★ ★ ★

21

At dinner, it seemed like my father had found his voice again. His face was red and flushed, and he kept insisting I agree with him that this house would solve all our problems. As was usual then, it was just the two of us, but finally it seemed to me that the strong, stoic man I knew — who could give me a greater sense of security than anyone else — had returned.

I replied that the house was beautiful and that I appreciated the effort he had put into getting it.

"Nonsense!" he replied. "It went for a few francs, with what's going on in Paris!"

I felt a pang in my heart. I knew nothing about what was happening in Paris, other than the little information my friend Lupin had included in his last letter, which was dated two weeks earlier by then.

"Is it dangerous?" I asked him.

"Dangerous? It's much more than dangerous. It's absurd! Imagine a pack of scoundrels influencing all the respectable people!" my father exclaimed. "That's what's happening. And if someone doesn't take charge again, it will get even worse."

"Worse than what?" I asked him.

"Worse, and that's enough! I told Gautier, too. The city's become an insane asylum! It needs Napoleon again, and it needs him in a hurry!" he thundered. But his eyes were smiling.

And so I held my own with that Papa who was once again so happy to talk to me about politics. And even though I did not really understand the topics he was talking about, the return of his good mood was enough to comfort me.

"Papa?" I said at the end of dinner, as our plates disappeared on a silver tray. "Before we got here, who lived in this house?"

He wiped his mouth with his napkin, crumpled it into a ball, and stared at it for a long time, as if it were an ancient treasure map. Finally he said something. "Shall we go say hello to your mother?"

Chapter 3

A LILAC-
COLORED ROOM

Our first week in Evreux was a good week.

There were four empty bedrooms on the top floor of the country home, but I chose a fifth, which was not a real room but rather the attic. It had whitewashed lime walls; strong, sloping beams looming at the ceiling; and a round window that faced the park, the bed of reeds, and the river bend. I helped Mr. Nelson carry up a mattress, which I eased onto the floor on top of a rug, to my father's horror. He once again tried to play the role of a worried parent.

"A young lady shouldn't —" he began, when I showed him the mattress on the floor and the lamp resting on a pile of books beside it.

I interrupted him, hugging him suddenly.

" . . . shouldn't bump her head every time she gets out of bed?" he finished instead.

"Don't worry, Papa! I'll be careful."

Indeed, the attic was spacious, but the ceiling was low. With any other bed, I would have wound up feeling suffocated. My father looked around with his shoulders slightly stooping forward. He examined the open trunk in a corner of the large room, and the dresses I had hung all around it, attaching the hangers directly into tiny gaps in the wood, like you might find in an eccentric fashion boutique.

He scratched his head. "I believe you urgently need a tutor," he muttered, bending over to climb down the narrow stairs.

"There's room in the house for one!" I replied cheerfully. I said this not because I wanted a tutor, but because my father had not opposed my idea of sleeping in the attic.

"Did you notice?" I asked Mr. Nelson when we were alone. "He said, 'Yes!'"

He was fussing with the windows overlooking the garden and then nodded, satisfied. "Did you check that they open quietly?" he asked me.

I joined him at the windows, surprised. "What did you say?"

"The windows," Mr. Nelson said. "They are quite old, and the hinges are rusty. You will want to make sure I can't hear you when you leave the estate secretly, Miss Irene, or when your good friends want to meet with you for some reason."

I jumped. How could he have known I intended to write Sherlock and Arsène?

Mr. Nelson peered through a windowpane, onto the sloping roof. "From here, it's not to be considered." He moved on to another window. "Not even from here . . ."

He stopped in front of the third window. "Maybe from here," he said. "The branch of the elm tree doesn't seem too far from the top of the gutter. Of course, you'll have to be very careful not to slip." He stared at me mockingly.

"What exactly are you saying to me, Mr. Nelson?" I asked.

"What am I saying to you in your opinion, Miss Irene?" he answered.

"I'm asking you," I replied.

"Ah. Very good . . ." Mr. Nelson pretended to scratch his chin thoughtfully. Then he crossed his arms over his chest and raised an eyebrow to underscore the irony of how much he trusted me. "I'm saying that once your first days of exploring the new house are over, you may want to leave on your own, as you usually did in London on Wednesdays and Fridays. Perhaps it would be better if your mother and your father didn't know about it. So as not to worry them, you understand. I must point out, in strict confidence, that it certainly won't be from me that they hear about it."

Mr. Nelson gestured to the attic around us. "But one would be able to guess from the creaking of the wood above one's head, from the windows that cannot be closed from the outside and, therefore, slam in the wind or, heaven forbid, from a branch or a gutter that suddenly collapsed under the weight of a personality as lively, so to speak, as yours, Miss Irene."

He ended all this with a wide grin that completely floored me. Never had he spoken to me like this.

I giggled nervously, because it seemed to me that he was somehow right. I found the attic magnificent because it was the most isolated and protected place in the house, but it was also the least accessible from outside. Mr.

Nelson was giving me the opportunity to decide how much I would want to bury myself in my things, my books, and my thoughts in that attic and how much, instead, I would want to choose a room below, which I could easily come and go from.

I hesitated, and he took advantage of it. "Did you notice the odd bay window in the small lilac bedroom, Miss Irene, the one in the corner of the house?"

"The one with the window covered by vines?" I asked.

"Yes," he replied. "The room with the tiny trapdoor."

My hands moved involuntarily, reaching to push my hair off my forehead. "Tiny trapdoor?"

"It's a bit rusty, yes. And I think it leads to an equally tiny spiral staircase, right in the middle of the vines . . ."

"Mr. Nelson?"

"What, Miss Irene?"

"Why are you telling me all this?"

"Because, as I told you, the tiny trapdoor creaks persistently, and even if you are careful, it will always squeak a little. And my room is the first one alongside the bay window. Supposing I should become aware of one of your excursions, I would prefer to know you're hidden among the leaves of the vines rather than dangling from a third-story gutter."

I looked at the attic around me — a quiet, open space. It felt like being enclosed in an ancient, wooden shell, creaky and resin-scented. I found it very difficult to think of giving it up.

"Who knows? Perhaps the time for excursions is over," I muttered. "After all, Evreux is a sleepy country village."

"The village may well be sleepy, Miss Irene, but you are not. We both know this."

Mr. Nelson climbed down the little wooden steps, making them creak. "Or better still . . . all four of us know!" he corrected himself after he had already disappeared from my sight.

I let go of my hair, which fell back on my face wildly.

"Have you already written your friends, miss?" Mr. Nelson asked me from the floor below, before moving away down the hallway.

As a result of this conversation, I decided to move into the lilac-colored bedroom, to the delight of Papa and Mama, who thought I was simply being less difficult.

And every once in a while, in the days to come, I heard them ask each other from the room where Mama was resting, "Did you hear that strange creaking?"

★ ★ ★

I sent the letters almost immediately. The one to my friend Sherlock Holmes left for London with the post the day after I moved into the lilac-colored room. The letter contained a brief recap of what had happened in the last few weeks, and also a request for several issues of the *Globe* — the London daily newspaper in which Holmes had a regular puzzle column. I sent my letter for Lupin to Brussels, where I knew the traveling circus in which he and his father, Theophraste, performed was currently stationed. Just to be certain, I made a copy. This I sent to Paris, to the address where, according to my friend, there was someone who acted as their agent and who, within a few weeks, I discovered to be the former Mrs. Lupin.

During the succeeding days, I tried to spend as much time as possible with my mother and got into the habit of reading to her every day from a novel. It was nice sharing a story with her, as I believed she had done for me when I was little. To tell the truth, it was a very distant memory, and a vague one, so much so that I did not recall a single one of those stories, nor even her voice. But there was something nonetheless familiar about reading aloud from a book at her bedside. I felt somewhat irritated when I found out my mama had chosen *Paul and Virginia*, an old novel by Bernadin de Saint-Pierre, which fit poorly with my taste for "scandalous" books by those American writers that Mr. Nelson secretly shared with me. I think that he and I, particularly, were the big readers in the Adler house.

I found Bernardin de Saint-Pierre's writing pompous and outdated, but my mother seemed to adore it. She stopped me from time to time to comment on this passage or that, frequently when there were touching scenes or preaching dialogues that she hoped in her heart would be useful to me.

If she only could have guessed that I loved the dark stories of Mr. Edgar Allan Poe, in which Detective Dupin hunted for a monkey killer!

These afternoons passed calmly, and I saw my mother's face slowly turn pink. After a week at Evreux, two hundred pages of a novel, and just as many small cups of beaten eggs, she found the strength to get out of bed and walk to her window that overlooked the river.

I followed a step behind her, afraid she might fall, watching her thin body, stiff under her bathrobe and fragile as a spider's web.

"What a splendid church, don't you think?" she asked after leaning against the windowpane to look outside for a long time.

Hers was perhaps the only window in the house from which you could see the bell towers of the cathedral through the trees.

"Well, it is . . ." I hesitated.

"You don't like it?"

"I find it . . ." I started, but the words wouldn't come. "Threatening."

"How strange," she murmured. "It makes me think how God must be."

"Pointy?" I joked.

But she didn't reply.

* * *

Luckily, Papa did not look for a tutor for me right away. Or perhaps he tried, but had no luck. My mother's illness had made my education less of a priority, and I had no intention of protesting.

I spent a good part of my days reading on the swing, on the wooden jetty, or hidden in the attic. I daydreamed and grew sad, feeling myself left to my own devices a little too often after the months spent in London and the intense events I'd experienced. I had risked my life in a den of thieves, crept into a theater in the company of a killer, spent time on the seediest streets and in the most disreputable places in the city, found myself face to face with agents from Scotland Yard, and been threatened with a pistol on the docks of the Thames. And, especially, I had been swept away by a kiss from one of my friends and had been hugged enthusiastically by the other of them.

The pain I felt from missing them both grew more pronounced across the distance.

So as not to lose touch with what my world had been over the previous months, I worked on my English by reading Mr. Nelson's books, having sworn I would not admit I had gotten them from him under any circumstances.

"You could say that you stole them from me, rather, or that they came from the public library in Evreux . . ." Mr. Nelson said.

At that idea, we both burst out laughing. To see if there was at least a library, we went together for a short walk in the country. We crossed the bridge and found ourselves in a small square with lovely little wooden houses facing it.

Wherever we walked, I felt the shadow of the cathedral above me, and when Mr. Nelson asked me if I would like to visit it, I refused. But there was a library in Evreux. It was tiny and only contained books in French, among which, I realized, there weren't many new ones. I borrowed a couple of small volumes by Mérimée, however, and explained to the lady at the counter that we had recently moved to the village.

"Ah, you're guests at poor Mr. d'Aurevilly's estate!" she said.

I hesitated and saw that Mr. Nelson was hesitating, too. The young lady wavered as well, as if she had said something awkward. She avoided meeting our eyes, as she had done from the moment we had entered. But I knew that she had really been scrutinizing the dark-skinned Mr. Nelson with curiosity every instant she thought she was not being observed.

"Why 'poor?'" I asked.

"Because he hasn't been back to Evreux for years. He and the foreign young lady who lived there," she murmured. "These days, the capital is dangerous for foreigners . . . and for all gentry, if they are born of old families like him, you understand."

Actually, I did not. I thought Papa had bought that country home and that we were not merely guests. But since I had noticed how the young lady spoke of the new Parisian government with venom in her voice, I tried to let her have her way.

"What scoundrels!" I exclaimed, expressing an opinion that wasn't mine.

"You said it, miss!"

"Or perhaps it would be better not to say just that," Mr. Nelson whispered, taking the books from the counter and accompanying me to the exit.

★ ★ ★

I thought that everyone had forgotten about me or that I even existed, and that my mother's illness had pushed us to the fringes of the world, to this place where not far from me — although out of reach — things did happen. I thought that the sleepy country spring would turn into a muggy marsh of boredom.

It seemed to me as if the seclusion of the d'Aurevilly house was like what Mrs. Brontë described when she said, "In all England, I do not believe that I could have fixed on a situation so completely removed from the stir of society." Except in that novel, the heroine shared her solitude with the man she loved, while I was spending my time in the company of books — mine and Mama's old novel. Surrounded by so much tranquility, I grew convinced that nothing exciting would happen to me until we left there.

However, nine days after we arrived in Evreux, I discovered I was wrong. Beneath the seat of my swing, I found a strange note written in a delicate feminine handwriting that I did not recognize.

Chapter 4

GRACEFUL
HANDWRITING

"Mr. Nelson?" I called, going back into the house. "Did someone arrive? Do we happen to have guests?"

It would not have been the first time that — shut up with my books and my thoughts — I was unaware someone had come, perhaps the village doctor or a colleague of Papa's.

Mr. Nelson was supervising the cleaning of the sitting room. He replied without ceasing to give orders to the household staff in grand style, scarcely moving a white-gloved hand. "Guests, Miss Irene? None today. Why do you ask?"

I stopped in the middle of the carpet, which I sank into almost up to my ankles. "Have you seen a gardener, perhaps? Or the mailman? Someone passing along the river?"

"Has something happened I should know about?" Mr. Nelson asked.

"Yes, maybe . . ."

I hid the note in my hand so he could not see it.

"Should I suspect something, Miss Irene?" he said without looking at me. "Or perhaps prepare the guest room? For one person? Or maybe two?"

I laughed. Certainly my two distant friends hadn't come this time.

"It's not what you think!" I replied, seeking refuge in my room.

"It's never what I think, Miss Irene," I heard him respond from his command post.

★ ★ ★

It was obvious that Lupin and Holmes had nothing to do with the note. To me it seemed certain that it had been written by a woman. The writing on the envelope was in a bluish color, sketched with a slanted hand:

To be delivered to Miss Irene Adler.

Inside the envelope was an ivory-colored card with a brief message:

I beg you to come to the cathedral garden this afternoon at four o'clock. I would like to tell you about Mr. d'Aurevilly and your mother.

That was all. I read it a second time, wondering what Mr. d'Aurevilly could have to do with my mother. Then I went to check the time on the pendulum clock. It was less than a half hour before four, a sign that whoever had delivered the note had expected me to find it much earlier.

Had it already been under my swing that morning? I wondered.

If Sherlock had been with me, he would certainly have been able to give me an answer, possibly figuring it out from the dampness of the envelope and the card. But Sherlock was on the other side of the sea, and the clock showed that it was past 3:30, so I did not think about it for long. I decided to leave the house right away, careful to pass by my mother's room to say goodbye first.

I found her standing, walking slowly from one side of her room to the other, as the doctor had recommended she do in order to regain the strength in her legs.

"I'm going to go for a walk into the village," I told her.

"What a splendid idea!" she replied. "I can't wait until I am able to go with you."

I bit my tongue, hesitating in the doorway to her room. "Mama?"

She looked at me. "What is it?"

"Nothing," I responded, rejecting the idea of asking her if she personally knew Mr. d'Aurevilly.

Without another word, I headed for the park.

★ ★ ★

The Evreux Cathedral seemed to capture every ray of light. It was made of light gray marble. The brightness of the marble contrasted with the shadows from the arches, pointy spires, and tall bell tower. The cathedral was supported by bold buttresses that made it look more like a rocky mountaintop than a place of prayer, at least to my eyes. And the large rose window in the front looked like a big eye staring at me instead of the flower its builders probably intended.

The village was as sleepy as ever. The few passersby loafed at the intersection of the two main streets, acting as if they had nowhere to go.

It was not hard for me to find the garden specified in the note. It was a green space beside the cathedral, divided into sections by spoke-like paths and the gravestones of local people. I spotted a bench and sat down, looking around.

I saw a family of crows perched on the spires of the cathedral like sentinels, and I followed their flight. They glided across the grass and pecked at the gravestones. They seemed to display a wicked familiarity, as if they knew better about the past, present, and future events in Evreux than anyone else.

"Forgive me for having asked you to come here," a woman's voice interrupted my thoughts at that point. The voice was both soft and deep. "I am truly sorry, Miss Irene."

I had been so focused on studying the crows that I had not realized a bejeweled woman had drawn near. She was a few steps away, staring at me.

I started with surprise. I stood up, embarrassed, but tried to act nonchalant. I could not figure out how that woman had been able to sneak into our garden all the way to my swing, leave the card for me, and then depart undisturbed.

"Don't worry about it. It's only a short distance," I replied. "If anything, I found your method of communication . . . intriguing."

"I know, I know. I can imagine it!" the woman said, sitting down next to me.

I could not see her eyes, which were hidden behind the veil of an elaborate little hat. I was amazed to note that her style of dressing, which would have been bizarre on any London street, seemed perfectly appropriate in an Evreux garden.

"May I at least ask who you are?" I began, but she was quicker than me.

"Poor little girl, poor treasure that you are . . . Your mother has told me so much about you!"

"My mother? You know her?" I asked.

"Oh, yes!" the woman replied. "I have known your mother for many years. I knew she had a lovely daughter, honest and intelligent. But to see you now before me and discover you are just as she said . . . Ah, believe me, it is truly thrilling!"

She went to pat me, but I pulled back instinctively, almost without being aware of it.

"Please excuse me, ma'am," I said, "but . . . you know I'm here because of a strange note."

"Yes, exactly. And thank you for coming, despite the times we live in."

"You mentioned my mother . . ."

The lady sighed, but she seemed to do so to buy time. It was strange — I felt no warmth from her, and yet it was as if there was something burning between us.

At that point, staring right at me, the lady pulled the veil away from her face. I studied her closely, but I did not recognize her. I had never seen her before.

"Your mother would probably kill me," the woman continued, whispering, "if she only knew I had come to you and what I intended to do. But I have to do it. And you, miss, will certainly forgive me for this bizarre request."

And then, in a faint voice, the lady with the pale eyes and broad, white forehead with a single wrinkle, begged me to return home to the d'Aurevilly house and retrieve an oilcloth envelope that was hidden behind a portrait in the library. She explained that the object had no monetary value, but that it was crucial it did not fall into the wrong hands. It would save Mr. d'Aurevilly, and as result, said the lady, my mother, too.

There seemed to be a number of holes in her story, not the least of which was her wanting to meet me, a young girl, in great secrecy, and promising a reward for delivering this precious envelope to her. But before I could even ask her a few of the questions that came to mind, her expression grew distressed, as if something worrisome had just occurred to her.

The woman stammered a couple of words quickly. "I — I'm sorry, but I must go," she said. "I beg you to believe me. That item is of utmost importance to me . . . Meet me tomorrow at this same place and same time. Farewell!"

Confused, I found myself staring at that strange person as she rushed away toward the cathedral. Just then, I noticed that a carriage had appeared over where the main street crossed the bridge and was lost in the countryside.

"Wait!" I cried, but it was too late. The woman pulled open the small side door of the cathedral and went in.

I ran after her. In the meantime, the carriage that had arrived from the countryside turned down one of the village lanes.

As soon as I flung the door open, I was hit with the organ's thundering chords. A dull, funereal song rose from the depths of the church. I staggered in the incense-rich air and leaned against a column. It was warm inside, and a service was taking place. The notes of the organ dissolved in the air, accompanying the choir, which was singing in Latin.

I felt short of breath. I searched in vain for the woman with the hat and veil among the faithful sitting in the pews. Thinking I heard the sound of her heels echoing along one of the naves, I anxiously followed it and found myself under the light of the rose window, completely paralyzed.

"What is this, here?" I whispered.

I went back out to the park and somehow forced myself to pass the time until mass was over.

When the main door opened, I stayed to watch all the faithful leaving for their homes. The sun began to sink behind my back, lengthening my shadow like a sad scarecrow.

I waited until no one else came out, but the woman with the blue handwriting did not leave the church. I had guessed she would.

What I could not have guessed would happen on a day like that was hearing the voice of my friend Arsène Lupin, instead. "Excuse me, miss, could you tell me where the Adlers live?" he asked me.

"ARSÈNE!" I shouted, overwhelmed with surprise and joy.

"I'm honored that you know me, miss," Lupin said, taking off his hat like the most seasoned of theatrical folk.

"But I was asking you about the Adlers. They're quite reserved. You may have met a tall, dark-skinned butler and an adorable young girl with red hair . . ."

"A sea of freckles," I think he also said, but I cannot be sure, because I suddenly found myself in his arms. I held him tightly, and he hugged me back. His skin was hot and smelled of sweat under his coarse shirt and waistcoat.

He kissed my hair and held my face between his hands, moving far enough away to look me directly in the eyes.

I could not believe it.

"How did you get here?" I asked him. As I asked him that, I wondered if Mr. Nelson had seen him this afternoon and if perhaps the note and the lady were nothing more than one of my friend Lupin's jokes. But there was enough time to look back at him and see that his gaze was somehow lost and desperate.

"I pedaled on my new boneshaker," he said, presenting me with one of his irresistible smiles.

I did not understand my feelings.

Even today, from the distance of so many years and after the thousands of adventures and encounters I have had, I cannot keep myself from hesitating as I write that yes, that day, in front of the Evreux Cathedral, with the blood-red sun shining between the hills and the river, it was I who kissed Arsène Lupin.

Perhaps my father was right. Perhaps I really did need a tutor. But like so many other things that should have happened, by then it was already too late.

Chapter 5

AN UNEXPECTED GUEST

"Remarkable. Truly remarkable!"

My father muttered words such as these for almost half an hour after Arsène Lupin showed him the bicycle he had ridden — alone and in a single day — across the ninety-six kilometers that separated us from Paris. "This boneshaker really is a marvel."

"You can say that again, Mr. Adler!" Arsène replied. "Entirely front-wheel drive, and look at those wheels — wood covered with a practically indestructible iron ring. It's just too bad that the backsides of those who ride it aren't made like that!"

My father looked puzzled, but Arsène went on. "It's a trouble on country roads, believe me. But on the smooth Parisian tarmac, which has no bumps, or at least what's left of it doesn't, I mean, you can go eighteen miles an hour!"

"Bah!"

"Try it, Mr. Adler, and tell me if I'm wrong!"

"So how much does this contraption weigh?" Papa asked.

"A trifling sixty pounds!"

They went on like this until Mr. Nelson announced that dinner was ready.

They completely ignored me, as if Arsène had not ridden all the way here after receiving my letter, but rather only to show my father this brand-new invention that would eventually transform the streets of Paris yet again. They acted like two children with a new toy, ready to compete with each other and take it apart. Mind you, it was a demon of a bicycle — a very heavy, rigid contraption, far from the fully developed, more comfortable models we would see in the streets in years to come. But perhaps that was exactly why Lupin's bicycle held such an appeal.

We sat down at the table, where my father took

advantage of my friend Lupin's arrival to get fresh news of Paris.

"It's just like what you'd imagine, sir," Lupin responded. "Everyone lives one day to the next in an atmosphere of great confusion. Mr. Thiers has declared that —"

"Mr. Thiers, eh?" my father interrupted. "He's now supposed to be governing? And whom did we put in charge of the schools?"

"They seem to want a woman, sir."

"A woman! Good God!"

"And excuse me, why not?" I broke in at that point, as the sole representative of the female gender. "May I ask what is so strange about entrusting a woman with the job of —"

"Please, Irene," my father muttered.

Lupin smirked at me.

"No, I really mean it, Papa!" I retorted. "Explain it to me. Explain why you think the job needs a man at any cost."

"Look —" he grumbled, much less exasperated than he wanted to appear.

"Do you think I wouldn't be capable of doing the same things as this . . . this . . . Thiers?!"

"As well as him? Well, of course, but that's little enough!"

"Papa!" I objected, but Arsène burst out laughing, unable to hold himself back.

"Arsène!" I shouted.

But both kept laughing. That mysterious male alliance had sprung between the two of them — an alliance that lets two men from even the farthest parts of the planet find a perfect reason to agree about something. And perhaps, a moment later, another perfect reason to wage war with their armies.

But I was not offended by their laughter. I had other things on my mind, and the fact that my father and Lupin were getting along allowed me to consider those things.

My thoughts revolved around that afternoon's meeting, the strange woman who said she knew my mother, and the task with which she had entrusted me. And also that kiss, which I thought Lupin and I would finally have to talk about once we were alone.

Instead, he seemed comfortable telling all sorts of other stories. Apparently his father, Theophraste, had finally settled down. He had opened a school for acrobats in the XII arrondissement, one of the neighborhoods in Paris.

"A school for acrobats?" my father groaned. "That's doomed to break down as soon as we have a self-respecting government again!"

"You bet, sir," Arsène replied. "But in the meantime, my poor father has found a post as a director and is very satisfied with it. He teaches children the sport in exchange for a modest payment, and in the evenings he holds long meetings discussing philosophy."

"Like every self-respecting Frenchman," Papa replied.

"My father is Belgian, sir. So for him, being listened to has a certain novelty."

"And what does your mother say about this? Is she happy about these meetings?"

I stiffened, thinking that Lupin would react poorly to this question.

It was not an easy subject, much like Sherlock's father was a difficult subject for him. These two figures were both absent in their children's lives. I only knew that Arsène's mother had been separated from Theophraste for many years and that Sherlock's father had died eight years before.

"I'd prefer not to speak of my mother if that's all right," Lupin amiably replied. And he did not touch on the subject again.

We clinked our glasses, and I proposed a toast and some dessert, which Mr. Nelson had brought out quickly. Then Papa took his leave and went to visit with Mama.

Lupin and I moved into the sitting room. "Mr. Nelson," he murmured, as he marched right under my butler's nose.

"It's a pleasure to see you again, Master Lupin. We were already into our second week of complete tranquility."

"You offend me, Mr. Nelson," Lupin retorted.

"Have you already found lodgings at the village inn?" asked Mr. Nelson.

"How did you guess?" he answered back.

"It's elementary, as your friend Master Holmes — whom I hope won't pop out from under the bushes right now — would say," Mr. Nelson said. "Your iron roadster has no luggage, nor a change of clothing. Thus I deduced you had already passed by there. But it's a pity. We've set up a comfortable room for guests in the attic, for unexpected events like this."

"There's really no need," Lupin said, laughing. "And my compliments for making those deductions. It would seem that our passion for investigating has become contagious!"

Mr. Nelson gave us a comic bow. In the middle of it, I thought he exchanged a few words with Lupin in a low voice. But I was facing away, so I could not be sure of it. Then Mr. Nelson cleared his throat. "May I bring you a nice hot tea or a small herbal digestive?"

When we were finally alone, I told Arsène everything, pausing only when Mr. Nelson brought us our drinks.

"Completely crazy!" Arsène exclaimed at the end of the tale. "And this envelope. Did you get it yet?"

"Actually, no," I admitted. "I haven't had time."

"What are we waiting for?" Lupin asked, leaping to his feet.

We headed toward the library in the house, trying to walk at a pace that was casual and calm. Once we went into the little reading room, I realized right away which portrait the woman was referring to. I approached it and pulled the frame away from the wall. Running my hand behind it, I found a small packet made of oilcloth wedged behind the frame.

Lupin was waiting for me in the doorway, half-heartedly admiring the watercolor landscapes that lined the hallway. In a moment, I was back next to him.

We returned to the sitting room, envelope tightly in my hand, and sat back down where we had been before.

Arsène sipped a splash of digestive, as if it were totally normal. And I thought that it was not so strange to see him here on the other side of the table after all. He was my good friend. He was one of my two best friends. And although my heart beat furiously — and confused me — I actually felt calmer. I realized that most of his boldness was just an act, and that he had to be even better than Sherlock at hiding his real feelings.

Shielded by the evening shadows, with the embers crackling in the fireplace beside us, sending reddish flashes into the sitting room, it seemed far nicer to me than I now recall.

I lowered my eyes right away, so as not to get even more confused. I wanted to say to him, "Do you know why I kissed you?" Instead, I pulled out the envelope and laid it on the table between us.

"Now what do we do?" I asked, staring at it.

"We open it, of course!" my impulsive friend responded.

I hesitated, uncertain. Then I pushed the envelope toward him, inviting him to continue.

"No," Lupin replied, amiably. "That could bring bad luck. You found it, and you open it." Smiling, he passed me a silver letter opener that I was certain had been in the hallway connecting the dining room with the sitting room a few moments before.

"Arsène!" I exclaimed. "If Mr. Nelson —"

"Shhh . . . It's just a little conjuring trick," Lupin whispered. "To stay in practice."

Sly, thieving, and unapologetic Arsène. I took my letter opener back from him and opened the envelope without another word.

"So?" he asked me, distracted by the embers in the hearth.

"So, I really don't know what to say . . ." I murmured, pulling a scrap of old, yellowed paper from the envelope. It was covered with meaningless lines. I looked at Lupin. "What is it, do you think?"

"Hanged if I know!" Lupin exclaimed, leaning over to see better. He looked at it for a long time, from one side and the other, and even through the light.

Then Arsène grew weary of it. Putting it on the table he said, "Do you know what?"

"Yes," I replied, because I understood. There was no need for us to say anything else.

There was only one person in the world who could get excited by a scrap of old, yellowed paper covered with meaningless lines.

"Will you write him?" Lupin asked me, jumping to his feet.

"I'll write him," I replied.

I went with him to the garden, where it had grown decidedly brisk. Lupin pointed to a small walkway hidden among the vines and asked if he could leave his bicycle there. The inn was just a few steps away from the center of town, and he did not feel comfortable riding at night.

"Of course," I responded, looking down at it. "See you tomorrow."

"See you tomorrow."

We made a couple of laughable movements, both of us stiff and awkward.

"Perhaps we should shake hands?" I laughed, by then completely embarrassed.

He laughed, too, and gave me a brotherly hug.

"I missed you," he said.

"Me, too," I replied. "It's good to see you here."

And we both were sincere.

I waited until he had gone through the gate before I went back into the house. I climbed up to the lilac room, my stomach in knots, and met Mr. Nelson coming down from the attic. He was carrying the stub of a candle in a candlestick.

"Is everything okay, Mr. Nelson?" I asked him, surprised.

"Everything is very good, miss," he replied, with no further explanation.

Chapter 6

THE RIVER

The next morning, a light drizzle fell and low clouds shrouded the countryside. A dull ringing filled my head. It had been a stormy night in which it seemed as if every piece of furniture in the house creaked and my covers were scorching hot. I had kept turning the heart-shaped, golden pendant that one of my two friends gave me for Christmas over and over in my hands. I'd tried lighting the gas fire many times to see it better. *It must have been from Lupin,* I kept repeating the whole night. Of course the gift had to have come from Lupin!

I rose and got the latest of my diaries — those same diaries that have allowed me to reconstruct my daring childhood today. I opened it to a certain page filled with cross-outs. During those first months of the year, every time I believed I could guess whether Arsène or Sherlock had given me that gift, I wrote down one of their names. By then, I had crossed out their names on the page twenty times.

That night I checked. And, as I had thought during the ebb and flow of my dreams, I had crossed out Sherlock's name for the umpteenth time and replaced it with that of Arsène. Only then, exhausted, did I fall asleep.

The morning passed slowly. I took refuge in my room, in the company of the pages of my beloved Le Fanu. I tried not to think of my afternoon appointment with the woman from the cathedral.

I did not even try to draft a letter for our friend, Sherlock Holmes. What could I write him? That I missed him? That Arsène and I wished he were with us? Why, then? Because we had an old piece of paper we could not decipher? I told myself that we did not have enough information to be able to ask for an opinion. And although in my heart I was dying for news from him, I put it off and sought refuge between the pages of *Uncle Silas*.

Lupin and I had agreed to meet at home right after lunch to decide what I should do before four o'clock.

Meanwhile, I could not help but rack my brains about that piece of paper — apparently meaningless and yet so carefully hidden in the house — and about the talk the woman had with me the day before. Her answers had not entirely convinced me, and I wondered whether I should show up for the afternoon appointment. I felt suspicion toward that strange woman and was reluctant to give her the envelope. Nonetheless, it made me deeply uncomfortable to keep something that someone had so urgently requested and that I had been told was so dangerous.

When Lupin finally turned up at our house in the afternoon, he had changed his clothes and put on a brand-new outfit that was a bit too large for him. He was also boasting a scent that was somehow familiar.

We went out into the garden and took a slow stroll, discussing what to do. We walked side by side, like astronomers discussing the marvels of creation. And in that moment, all the events and the meeting of the day before seemed distant, as if I had experienced them in a dream or read about them in a book.

"What I can't figure out," Lupin interrupted all of a sudden, "is why this lady didn't get the owner of the house to write a note authorizing her to retrieve the letter. That's what I would have done in her place. How else does she think she can get it delivered to her based solely on her word?"

"That's what I asked her, to tell the truth. She replied that d'Aurevilly was very ill and is no longer rational. She hinted at some relatives who wanted to seize the estate and the fact that the housekeeper was in cahoots with them. Quite a vague story, actually. It struck me as suspicious."

We concluded that we knew too little to make a decision, and that the only possibility was to go meet with the woman so that we could at least ask for some explanations.

We headed toward the village with determined steps. The sweet smell of warm bread and raisins wafted through the alleys of the old village, between the cone-shaped roofs of the small castle and the medieval houses that had survived the revolution.

We reached the bench where I'd sat the previous day a few minutes before four. We sat down to wait, trying to talk about other things.

The bell towers chimed four o'clock, and then half past. We looked at each other, shocked, as it was twenty minutes to five by then.

Lupin rose. "Let's go," he said firmly. "I don't think a young lady like you should have to waste her time waiting for a bizarre woman who tells vague stories."

So saying, Arsène offered me his arm, and we prepared to go back home.

As we walked through the village, we reviewed what had happened to me the day before step by step, searching for a detail that I might have missed.

"Exactly when did the woman begin to act afraid?" Lupin asked at one point in the discussion.

But I could not tell him. I had not noticed anything strange around us then — nothing at all.

Only then did I remember the carriage that had approached on the main street of the village. And suddenly, that image made me think of the unusual carriage I had spotted on the streets of London last Christmas. When I was going to the Shackleton Coffee House — my friends' and my favorite cafe during that London winter — the carriage had come alongside me and a mysterious woman leaned out to give me a little Christmas gift.

"Nothing strange . . . at least, I don't think so," I muttered. "Only an approaching carriage that came into the village shortly thereafter."

Lupin stuck his hands in his pockets and led us toward the river. "And then there's what she said about your mother, that she had known her for many years . . ." he trailed off.

"And that she would be in danger," I said.

"You haven't yet spoken to her, of course."

"I didn't think it would be a good idea," I admitted. "And not just because of how she has been feeling at the moment, but because I think it would worry her too much, in any case."

Lupin seemed to agree with me. "Your mother is from here?" he asked.

"No," I replied.

"But she's French?" he asked.

"Yes, from Fontainebleau, just south of Paris.

"I know it. Where the palace is."

"But I've never been there. My mother did not particularly like going back," I said. "She liked being in Paris. Only in Paris, to be precise."

He made a hard face, which I quickly understood the reason for. We were both convinced we had to deal with demanding Parisian mothers, both of them a bit too pampered and incompetent. But instead, as the facts soon showed, neither of us was right to believe this.

"She said if your mother knew what she was doing, she'd kill her," my friend continued. "But the word *kill* is very odd for a lady to use," he observed. "She could have used an expression like *take steps* or *be annoyed about it*. But *kill*? Doesn't that seem a bit too . . . strong?"

I nodded. And that observation reminded me that the woman had seemed to be playing a part, like an actress.

I was about to tell Lupin so, when at that exact moment, a hand grabbed my by the shoulder and yanked me to the ground.

I screamed, but a second hand pressed over my mouth to stop me. Then it pulled down my collar, grabbed my gold pendant, and tore it off me. I felt my skin sting and kicked at my assailant, barely missing him.

I wound up flipped upside down, just as something sparkling fell to the ground. It ricocheted two steps in front of me with a metallic clink. A knife.

"Irene!" Lupin shouted.

He threw himself at my attacker like a lightning bolt, shoving him away. Then he stepped between a second man and me. The man was kneeling on the ground, holding a bloody hand and cursing in a low voice.

Lupin balanced from one foot to the other like a juggler. He did not seem at all intimidated by having to face two men considerably bigger than himself. One of them threw a punch, but Arsène dodged the blow and delivered a kick to his ribs. I heard him exhale like a bull, and I got back up.

"Are you okay?" my friend asked me, without glancing away from our attackers.

"Yes!" I replied, then I felt my neck. "The pendant! They stole it from me!"

"The young lady's pendant!" Lupin cried out.

"Hit him!" shouted the man with the bloody hand.

The other man hesitated, and that hesitation was crucial for us. Lupin had continued to retreat toward the river and I with him. When he heard those words, he did not wait a moment longer. He seized my wrist and pulled me into the current.

I found myself imprisoned by my dress, being dragged to the bottom of the river. With a rush of air, I kicked with all my might and returned to the surface about ten meters farther downstream from where we had been attacked. I tried to get to where the current was weaker, and then I saw that Lupin was swimming beside me.

Without a word, we crossed the river and climbed back up by the reeds along the opposite bank. Dripping, we headed toward the d'Aurevilly home.

I felt Arsène's arm supporting me and looked at him. He was still keeping a close watch to make sure those hoodlums weren't following us.

"All okay?" he asked me.

"Yes, but . . . what's going on?"

Chapter 7

REVISIONS

The candle burned quickly, as if there was a current of air flowing through the bay window, stretching the flame. It sat on the ground, beside the pages scattered across the floor. Lots of them, all wadded up and thrown away. Abrupt cross-outs and the sentences I could not finish stood out on all of them.

Dearest Sherlock . . .

All the pages began that way. And they continued in as many different ways as possible, until I felt ridiculous enough to stop writing, reread what I had tossed away already, and start over. The attack I had suffered that afternoon had finally convinced me to write to him, but that was not why I wanted to be clear about what I said to him.

Looking back, I must have felt vaguely in danger, but I would never have admitted it to myself then. Why would I tell Sherlock that a strange woman approached me in the park, claiming to know my mother? In our long conversations, Sherlock Holmes and I had spoken about many, many things, but practically never about either of our families. It was as if the subject was taboo for both of us.

At that time, as I probably have already written, I was convinced my family was not my real family. But even though the events to follow provided the proof, I could never actually have explained why I was so certain.

I think it had something to do with what happens to many young people the age I was then, especially if they are stubborn and a bit rebellious — as I was. Those moments of complete misunderstanding, in which the distance between oneself and one's own parents seems profound.

I had always perceived this distance between my mother and I, and I had grown up convinced that I was not really her daughter. But it was a completely private feeling I had — and it did not even occur to me that others might share it.

Therefore, that day in Evreux, faced by a woman who spoke about my mother, I did not doubt for a moment that it could refer to anyone other than Mrs. Genevieve Adler. The mother with whom I had spent all my years, at least as far back as I could remember anything, and who was now recovering from a lung infection a few rooms away from me.

It is strange how young people think, but that is exactly how it was for me those days. And that confusion in my thoughts was one of the reasons all three of us risked our lives as we had never done up to then.

And if I now write *all three of us*, it is because I did finally manage to finish my letter to Sherlock Holmes that night.

I sealed it and gave it to Mr. Nelson, who hid it in the pocket of his big jacket, with an expression of agreement and understanding.

The letter left that same morning with the fastest postal carrier, and I spoke about it with Lupin that afternoon.

"It seems like it may be a bit difficult for the letter to get to him with what's going on in Paris," my friend commented. "But you did well to let him know anyway. In case something should happen to us."

What could happen, of course, was not clear to either of us. And we racked our brains to understand the recent days' events.

"If you'd like, I'll go speak to your mother," Lupin offered at one point.

I stopped him from doing so, and he did not insist. He never commented on the theft of the pendant, nor asked me if it had any special value besides the gold it was made from. For my part, I was careful not to examine why he was so quiet.

"Arsène?" I said when evening fell and he said goodbye to me, in order to return to the inn where he said he was staying.

Long, gray clouds cut through the evening sky. The late winter sun had already set, and soon nearly everything would turn dark.

"What is it?" he said.

The air quivered as if a swarm of invisible insects had risen from the bushes.

"Has it ever happened, when you think of me or see me . . ." I hesitated.

"What?"

"I don't know," I continued.

And I really did not.

"It's like . . . I don't know . . . a little strange?"

Lupin moved his head back, as if to avoid a blow. He smiled. "Strange in what way?"

I felt stupid to have asked that question. Stupid and naïve.

Why would he ever have felt strange? I wondered, looking down at the ground as if I were at the edge of a precipice.

And what was the name of that girl who had left everything to join the circus, that girl who only a few months earlier I had been insanely jealous of?

"Forget it," I answered brusquely.

I went back into the house.

★ ★ ★

My mother's health improved before my eyes, and with her, the weather in Evreux. The clouds decreased and then faded away, and the days grew longer.

I stayed closed up in the house, reading to Mama and receiving Arsène's daily visits. He became our permanent dinner guest. My father liked my bold friend. And in her room, my mother asked me about him.

I did, however, hear a faint concern in her voice sometimes, and her questions were often mysterious.

For this reason, I tried to avoid them as much as possible, restricting myself to reassuring her of the fact that there was nothing between Lupin and me beyond a good friendship. Nonetheless, the fact that the boy was staying at an inn without his parents watching over him seemed abnormal to my mother, and with each passing day, her worry grew more pressing.

Having recovered a bit of energy, my mother began to consider whom among her friends in Paris she could write to, ask for news, and possibly send an invitation to visit our estate in the country. I took advantage of this opportunity to ask if she had ever known the former owner of the house in which we were staying, Mr. d'Aurevilly.

"I believe d'Aurevilly is or was one of your father's clients," she replied.

I asked Papa the same question at dinner.

"No. I never met him," he responded. "But we were put in touch with each other through mutual friends."

"It's a small world," Lupin commented, which led us away from the subject.

And that was a mistake, because had I found out more about the mutual friends Papa mentioned, perhaps I would have acted differently. Instead, I felt as if I were surrounded by shadows. And as if none of us had a lantern bright enough to dispel them.

★ ★ ★

I hastened to update Mr. Nelson about the attack at the river, begging him not to tell anyone a word about it. His response was to the point. "When you're alone, Miss Irene, these things never happen."

It had been clear to me that he disapproved of my friends' visits and that sooner or later, Lupin and I would have to meet secretly. Mr. Nelson certainly knew more than he let on.

The next day, Mr. Nelson appeared at the end of the hallway with a sly expression on his face, looking like a playful cat.

"We have guests, Miss Irene," he began, raising his eyebrows high.

"And Papa can't receive them?"

"I don't believe it would be appropriate," he responded.

"Ah," I remarked, thinking Mr. Nelson was talking about Arsène's visit.

I stupidly hoped Lupin had changed his clothes. Since he had arrived in Evreux, I had only seen him in one outfit. It fit him poorly, too, which my mother had pointed out.

"He says he's here for a game of chess," Mr. Nelson continued, mocking me even more.

I was caught off guard. "And what does chess have to do with us?"

"That's what I asked him. Even though, reading the labels on his luggage, I would say he should have been heading to Brussels."

"Brussels, Mr. Nelson? What are you trying to tell me?" I asked. "What guest could have come to Evreux who should have instead . . ."

I heard the clatter of Lupin's boneshaker on the path to the house and realized right away that the guest could not be him.

"From what I can gather, Miss Irene, your guest seems to have departed from London," the cunning Mr. Nelson concluded, plunging his hands into his waistcoat pockets. "Should I let him know you intend to receive him, or else —"

"Sherlock!" I cried out, moving past Mr. Nelson and catapulting myself down the stairs. "I can't believe it . . . Sherlock!"

"Irene? Horatio?" my mother's weak voice asked, from the room she was a prisoner of.

I let Mr. Nelson reassure her.

I ran down, crossed the foyer of the house and, with a leap, found myself in Sherlock Holmes's arms.

His odd checkered cap spun to the ground. I could not help but notice that after being so stubborn, he had finally bought it.

"Truly remarkable," Sherlock said, seemingly calm but wrapping me in a tight embrace. I do not know, however, if he was referring to the welcome or to Lupin's boneshaker.

★ ★ ★

That evening, both my friends were guests at the house. It was Sherlock's turn to explain to my father that he had joined us after a chess tournament in Brussels.

"I don't believe we're on the way to Brussels," my father commented.

"You're perfectly right, Mr. Adler," Sherlock responded. "But reimbursement for all the expenses of the trip was already arranged and . . . well, I hate to admit it, but I was eliminated in the first match. And since I was expecting to stay on the continent for an entire week, it seemed like a good idea to go find my friends."

"Who by a lucky coincidence are both here," my father smiled. His sly expression greatly reminded me of Mr. Nelson's.

"Precisely," Sherlock said. "And, therefore, what could be better than a visit to the lively French countryside, along the outskirts of a war that's far from finished — not to mention a looming civil war — rather than returning to London? I considered the pros and cons, Mr. Adler, and felt that a couple of days here wouldn't be a real problem for anyone. All the rooms at the only inn in the village, the Stag's Inn, were —"

I heard a dull thud, followed by wood creaking. Sherlock responded with a sudden silence, which drew Papa's attention.

"It seems wrong to send you to the inn, young Holmes, after the journey you've had," my father said. "And I don't think that our Arsène would have anything against it if we invited you to sleep in the house this evening."

Lupin looked like a wax statue, and I no less so. "Sleep here?" I said.

"Of course, Irene," Papa responded. "There should be a room in the attic for chance guests, if I am not mistaken."

"You're not mistaken, sir," Mr. Nelson broke in, clearing the plates off the table. "I will see to it myself, as soon as dinner is over."

"Splendid!" my father said, raising his wine glass up high. "Let's drink to youth! And to friendship!"

And so I did, confused and happy, because once again I was with all the members of my family.

★ ★ ★

"Let me see this piece of paper," Sherlock said right away, once we had finished our dinner and settled in the sitting room. No sooner had I handed him the old, yellowed parchment than he seemed entranced by it.

He carefully studied it, slowly and hungrily, while Lupin and I exchanged questioning looks. Our worry, along with our hope, was that in a few seconds he would be able to figure out more than we had — we who'd had it in our hands for almost a week.

"Right, of course. But only a part," Sherlock muttered, when the darkness in the sitting room forced him to look away.

"What?"

"Follow this outline and this line . . . do you see it here? They make a right angle, and then they go off the parchment in this direction. There's no doubt. It's part of a map."

"And what are we to do with a part of map?" Lupin asked.

"This we need to ask the hoodlums who assaulted you," Sherlock responded.

"They stole my pendant," I said.

"But they didn't say that was what they were looking for . . ." Sherlock replied.

"You're saying?"

"I'm not saying anything. But there are some things that do not add up. The woman at the cathedral who got lost in the crowd, running away as soon as she saw a certain carriage arriving, and then those two who suddenly appeared."

"How do you know these things?" Arsène burst out, amused.

"I write good letters," I replied.

"And I read those letters, unlike some other people," Sherlock said.

Arsène spread his arms out wide. "I would, too, but I move too quickly, my friends."

We stopped, because Mr. Nelson had opened the door to the sitting room. "The attic is ready, Master Holmes," he announced.

"Thank you very much, Mr. Nelson," Sherlock responded.

Then he turned to look at me and Lupin. "Tomorrow," he said.

"Tomorrow, what?" I asked.

"Tomorrow, the three of us start our counterattack."

Chapter 8

SNAPS AND SECRETS

I could not sleep. No matter how hard I tried to stuff my head under my pillow, I still could hear the ceiling creak. I realized it was the steps of Sherlock Holmes, who must've been as restless as I was. The night was a solid blanket above the park, and my bed shone a vibrant pearly gray, like a raft at the mercy of the waves.

I grumbled a bit, but eventually I gave up. I slipped out from under the covers and put a long woolen robe over my nightgown. I slid on a pair of thick socks and carefully padded out the door of my lilac room. Passing by Papa's room, I could hear his heavy breathing and the crumpling of his sheets every now and again. All that filtered out from Mama's room was a delicate silence. I leaned my foot on the first step to the attic and cautiously put my weight onto it.

Mr. Nelson had been right to dissuade me from choosing the attic for my bedroom. It was impossible to move around in it secretly, and it would have been difficult to sneak out of the house from there. I slowly climbed up the stairs, one step at a time, thinking back to why Mr. Nelson had convinced me to choose a room with a trapdoor and secret steps that led to the vines, since I knew he really hadn't wanted me to have a way to get into trouble.

I crouched in the shadows, dropping onto all fours to make the least amount of noise. But the wood seemed alive under my hands, and it creaked unpredictably.

Somehow I reached the door to the attic. Once there, I was about to knock when I was forced to stop, surprised. I heard Sherlock Holmes's voice faintly coming from the other side.

He was speaking to someone.

"These few hairs left on the pillowcase are enough for me to figure out who's been sleeping here," my friend was saying. "Are you sure that the others know nothing about it?"

"It was Mr. Nelson who suggested it to me."

"He knew that you'd run away from home then?" Sherlock asked.

"Just by looking at me."

"While Irene and her father think you're staying at the village inn."

"That's why I kicked you at dinner."

Only then did I recognize that the voice answering Holmes belonged to Lupin. So Mr. Nelson had been letting him sleep in the attic all along?

I squeezed even closer to the door.

"Is it a bad business, what your father's up to?" Sherlock asked.

"He says it's an opportunity to start fresh," Lupin said, "but I don't agree. I don't like the friends who got in touch with him in Paris and even less what they proposed he do. The city's in chaos, and my father . . . has a clouded past, as you know."

"But that's not what's really bothering you."

"No," Lupin admitted. "The problem is that he kept getting angrier and angrier at me. We were fighting about everything, and the moments of peace between one fight and the next were getting shorter. Was it like that with your father, too?"

"I'd say not, from what I remember," Sherlock said. "The word *fight* wasn't part of his vocabulary. That would suppose he even realized that other people existed, to mistreat them at all. No, my father never fought with anyone, but that's not why there was peace in the family, as far as I know. My mother is silent when Mycroft and I try to talk about it. It is my brother and I who are responsible for our family. Mycroft has almost finished his studies and wants to be a lawyer or a politician, with a chance of earning a decent living. I think it's a good idea and that he has a flair for it. Whereas I —"

Lupin snickered. "You want nothing to do with it."

"That career doesn't attract me at all. I'd rather become a mathematician, a concert pianist . . . or a violinist! But I feel like it won't entirely be my choice."

"At least you've got a brother," Lupin said.

"You're forgetting my little sister."

"Exactly — you'll never be alone. But I'm an only son."

"And your mother?" Sherlock asked.

"Oh, it's been five years since I went to see her."

"Why?"

"You can't imagine how cruel she can be. As if she had never forgiven herself for having had a son, and for having had one with my father. I think it was even out of spite toward her that my father let his new friends convince him to —"

Without any warning, the door I was leaning on suddenly opened wide. I fell into the room with a stifled little scream.

"Hello, Irene," Sherlock Holmes greeted me, kneeling in front of me. "Do you want to come in and make yourself more comfortable?"

"It's not what you think!" I hurried to explain myself. "I wasn't eavesdropping."

"It's never what you think it is," Lupin said, perched on the edge of his bed like a crow. He was dressed in his grubby nightclothes. Right then I realized why his clothes seemed familiar to me — they were ones my father had discarded.

All three of us sat down on the ground, with a candle lit between us. Wax cascaded down it.

"Truth is like a moth," Sherlock said. "When light comes, it disappears."

Lupin slipped his bare feet under a blanket. He looked thinner and younger than usual. "I think the three of us should do something," he murmured.

"What do you mean?" I asked.

"Trust," said Lupin. "We desperately need some trust."

"And we don't have it?"

Lupin grimaced. "We know we want to have it, but we're surrounded by people who are lying. And that's why we keep searching."

"Speak for yourself," I interrupted.

"Because you don't feel surrounded by lies, big and small? Or perhaps was it your idea to put me up in your attic secretly?" Lupin asked.

"I didn't suspect a thing," I said.

"Which means Mr. Nelson lied to you. And your father? And your mother? Are you really sure everything they tell you is true?"

"Yes," I lied.

"Or perhaps," said Lupin, "the truth is that we keep solving mysteries because we actually enjoy lies. Just a moment ago, I was hiding in this attic, Irene was behind the door, and you, Sherlock, where were you hiding?"

"In my head," he replied, his expression pensive and bleak.

We were silent for a while, as if we'd discovered something important. I was captivated by the mysterious power of the night, which made it all seem grander.

"I think we should take an oath," I said at that point, worried by hundreds of questions. "And swear that we will be different."

They looked at me.

"We should swear to tell each other the truth from now on," I said. "Always and no matter what."

They stared at me.

"Just us three," I added softly.

Then I brought the palm of my hand toward the lit candle. Arsène put his on top of mine, and Sherlock did so, too. We interlaced our fingers and held them above the flame until our skin burned from it. And that was how Sherlock, Lupin, and I sealed our oath of eternal trust in the attic of the d'Aurevilly house, in March of 1871.

It was our last oath as children — a naïve but powerful promise. It was a promise we could never turn back from. If even one of us broke it, all three of us would be forced to grow distant from each other forever.

And to grow up.

* * *

The next day, a pale, uncertain sun rose over Evreux. Sherlock and I met Lupin at the bridge. Lupin pretended to come toward us from the village, not knowing which mysterious observer this might benefit, given that my

father and mother were nicely shut up in the warmth of
the house.

"Plans?" he asked.

"The usual — the scene of the crime," Sherlock
replied. He handed Arsène one of the hot rolls he had
nabbed from the breakfast table, and Lupin munched on
it as we went into the village.

"How do you come and go from the attic discreetly?"
I asked him.

"Discreet isn't the best word to describe it," Arsène
joked. "Because sometimes I have a bad time of it with
the gutter. Let's just say that I take advantage of that tree
closest to the rooftop. Once there, it's easy enough."

We reached the spot along the walk where we had
been attacked a few days before and stopped there.

"The chances of finding something interesting here
are practically nil," Lupin said.

"Indeed. You should have come back right afterward
to check," Sherlock said.

I felt my neck ache. "It's not particularly easy when
someone has attacked you and tried to rob you!"

"I didn't say it was easy."

We set to searching with our eyes fixed on the ground,
dividing the area into zones. Luckily, no one passed by.

"What exactly are we looking for?" Lupin asked after about ten minutes of unsuccessful searching.

"If we knew, we wouldn't be looking," Sherlock replied, kneeling on the ground and examining the grass with his utmost concentration.

"Maybe . . . a button?" I asked, recovering a small object from behind a brick that had broken off from those that made up the embankment. I held it out between my fingers and showed it to my two friends.

"That's not a button," Lupin said. "It's too small."

"From a shirt?" I guessed, holding it to the light.

"It's a fastener from a shoe," Sherlock Holmes replied.

"Splendid," Lupin grumbled. "Now we have a trail."

Sherlock gave him a surprised look. "Well," he commented. "I'd say we do."

"And exactly how, for heaven's sake?"

Chapter 9

A GOOD REPAIR

"Is anyone here?" I asked, pushing open the door.

Inside, the shoemaker's shop was shrouded in shadows. Leather in different colors was nailed to the once-white walls, along with dark iron tools. On the counter sat long-handled wooden forms in the shape of feet, along with scissors and hammers, punches for making holes in leather, and colored string. A weak fire burned at the rear of the shop in the soot-covered fireplace.

A little man bent in two by his waistcoat approached me. His arms were long and his hands gnarled. "What can I do for you, *mademoiselle*?" he asked with a perfect Parisian accent.

"I don't exactly know," I replied, following the instructions Sherlock had given me. "But I found this and . . . I thought it could possibly be useful to you."

Saying this, I handed him the little snap we'd found at the river. The cobbler held it in his palm, staring at it carefully. And just as Sherlock had thought, he recognized it. It was the snap to an unusual fastener for a shoe.

"This is so lucky!" the shoemaker exclaimed.

"Really?" I said.

"Oh, yes. I thought it would drive me insane!"

"Seriously?"

"Yes, indeed," he said. "A customer came in a few days ago, asking me to repair a pair of boots with this snap. I asked to have several days to fix them, but until now I hadn't been able to find a fastener that matched the others. I was going to have to deal with it this morning no matter what, because the gentleman is coming to pick them up today."

"Do you still have them here?" I asked.

"Yes, it's these. Do you see?" he said, pointing to a pair of boots. "Without the fastener you just brought back to me, I was going to have to replace all of them. Do you see this hammered metal along the edge here? It's a fastener that's the latest fashion — comes straight from

Paris. One of those inventions we go crazy for, here in the provinces."

"And who is this man who is so alert to fashion, here in Evreux?" I asked.

The cobbler seemed captivated by the snap. "Would you believe? I don't know," he replied. "It was the first time he'd come into the shop."

* * *

We stationed ourselves nearby, careful to remain out of sight. Sherlock and Lupin had a deck of cards that they used to while away the time. I went home for lunch and reported back to the shoemaker's alley a little before two o'clock. At three, the shoemaker finally stopped hammering. Shortly after, as if he had heard, a curly-haired man in a very elegant overcoat appeared at the shop.

Lupin hid the cards in his pocket. Sherlock pulled his checkered hat down on his head. A few minutes after he went in, the man left, quickly walking in the opposite direction from the one he'd originally come from.

He was wearing the boots.

We followed him at a safe distance and left the village with him, passing into the countryside. The man was moving at a brisk but calm pace. He never turned back, as if he felt completely secure. He turned down a couple of increasingly narrow streets. After less than a half hour of walking, he arrived at a wooden barn, from which the roofs of Evreux could barely be seen.

"I'd say we're there," whispered Sherlock, who was walking ahead of us.

We crouched between the bushes and stayed there for a little while to watch. As soon as we were sure there was no one else nearby, we raced up to the side of the barn and began skirting it, looking for a way to get inside.

Arsène pointed out a small window on the upper floor and a wooden ladder carelessly propped up nearby. Moving it very carefully, we leaned it against the wall without making any noise. Sherlock crept up first, then I climbed up second, and Lupin followed us.

We crawled into a dusty, rickety loft. There were cracks between one board and the next, which let us see into the barn below. Sherlock led the way until we heard several men's voices chatting a few meters below us.

"Our orders were clear, Marcel!" one of them shouted. "We were supposed to tear up that cursed piece of paper!"

"And that's what I tried to do!" Marcel replied. "But she reacted like a panther!"

I couldn't hold back a smug grin.

"Why do I always have to work with a bungler like you? Why?" the first one said. I saw him wave my heart-shaped pendant and then throw it into the center of the room. "Why'd you think she'd wear it around her neck?"

"The thing glittered," Marcel said. "And besides, what do I know about what girls put around their necks? She could've put the folded-up paper in it, as far as I knew."

"If it wouldn't be a waste of the rope, I'd strangle you! Couldn't we make better use of a knife and finish the job, once and for all?"

"Enough already!" a third voice roared. Through the boards, I saw it belonged to the man who had picked up the boots. "What's done is done. Which is nothing at all."

"Look, I tried to get into that house at least twice, Bernache."

"And both times, you were forced to stop because of that mysterious knight."

"I swear to you, Bernache, it's a monkey! If you'd seen how it climbed up the tree and then onto the roof! It was impossible to get in there."

This time it was Lupin's turn for a smug grin.

"They smelled a rat, I'm telling you. The house is monitored."

"How scary."

"The guy who climbed onto the roof stabbed Marcel."

"And there's also the butler," Marcel added, coughing.

"As you wish, but we've got to have that piece of paper. And I have to take it to Saint-Vigor, to Mr. Montmorency."

"And we're telling you, Bernache, if you want that piece of paper, you've got to give us guns."

Lying down on the boards in the barn, Sherlock, Lupin, and I looked at each other, alarmed.

"Without guns, we aren't going back in there."

"And even with guns, you'll have to pound away, because —"

"Because you're a pack of bunglers!" Bernache yelled. "You only had to steal some parchment from a little girl! And you —"

CRACK!

It was one of the boards I was lying on. Before I could even curse, the entire section of the ceiling we were resting on opened up below us.

CRA-CRA-CRA-CRACK!

It was a fall of a few meters, and the debris fell onto one of the crooks below. I landed on something soft, which did me no harm at all. By time I stood up, Sherlock and Lupin had already jumped down after me.

"There they are!"

"It's them!"

"Look out!"

The two men I had not knocked down with my entrance started screaming, "Stop them!"

I saw Bernache fumble under his coat and pull out a long black object. Sherlock jabbed him with his elbow, and a gunshot went high into the rotted wood ceiling.

"Let's get out of here!" I shouted.

We got to the exit amid an uproar of screams.

"Not along the street!" Arsène screamed. "This way!" He dashed into the muddy, wet fields.

We ran with our hearts in our throats, getting farther and farther away from those hoodlums. Only when the barn was a tiny dot in the distance did we slow down.

Our clothes were filthy up to our knees, our faces were spattered with mud . . . and all three of us were laughing like lunatics.

We hugged each other, making sure we were all okay.

"Did you see them?" Sherlock asked, laughing.

"The panther!" I exclaimed.

"The roof monkey!" Lupin said.

Sherlock coughed, catching his breath. Then he added, "Whoever this Mr. Montmorency is, he's put together a team of genuine imbeciles."

Arsène pointed to his chest. "They were afraid of me! Do you realize? And there were three of them!"

"And of Mr. Nelson!" I chortled.

"And Irene's only answer was to put one of them out of action by diving onto him!"

Laughing, we staggered back to the d'Aurevilly house, completely soaked and sneezing in chorus.

"Good Lord," Mr. Nelson remarked when he opened the door for us. He stood still, blocking the doorway. "Take the secret stairs," he whispered.

Meanwhile I heard my mother's voice asking behind him, "Who is it, Horatio?"

"No one, madam!" he replied. "No one!"

We clambered to my room via the hidden stairs. Once there, we hid our wet clothes in a large sack. Trying not to make noise, I gave each of my friends a robe and took one for myself. Thus cloaked, we sought refuge in the attic.

"I don't even want to ask what happened to you," Mr. Nelson said a few minutes later. He was carrying a huge tub of hot water, which he had us soak our feet in right away. "Nor what trouble you've gotten into."

"Mr. Nelson —" I began.

"Not one word, Miss Irene."

"Listen —" Lupin started.

"And as for you two gentlemen," Mr. Nelson said, "it would behoove you both to sit there quietly, so that I don't go telling your families about whatever exploits you've recently undertaken."

He poured something pungent into the water and began massaging our calves vigorously without a word. Even though it was a treatment for avoiding colds, it seemed very much like torture. When he decided he was done, he looked at each of us one at a time with such an air of reprimand that I could not help burst out laughing.

"Do you find something funny, Miss Irene?" he asked.

"I'm very sorry, Mr. Nelson. We'll tell you everything, if you wish," I said.

"I insist on it, as the price of my silence."

Both Sherlock and Lupin nodded faintly.

"Okay . . . I think this time we really need you," I said.

"Need me for exactly what?" Mr. Nelson asked.

"Do you know where the village of Saint-Vigor is?" Lupin asked him.

"No," Mr. Nelson replied.

"Then we'll need someone else, too," Sherlock concluded.

Chapter 10

THE MONTMORENCYS

During the carriage ride to Saint-Vigor, I read about the Montmorency family in the *Almanac of Gotha*, a small book printed in Thuringia. They were one of the oldest families of the French aristocracy. The *Almanac* contained a brief history and a short list of their properties, which included the one we were going to.

"I really can't understand what . . . ACHOOO! . . . a nobleman like that could want from me," I remarked after I finished reading the book.

"I'd say your part of the map," Sherlock replied, concentrating on the countryside around us.

"Then let him have it!" I held back a second sneeze and added, "Besides, it's *not* my part of the map. Until a few days ago, I didn't even know it existed!"

"And that's really strange," Lupin agreed. "It seems like the woman who asked you so mysteriously to get it for her shouldn't have lost interest, leaving you right in the middle of this shady business."

Sherlock made a face, which didn't escape me.

"You don't believe it?" I asked him.

"I think there's something we don't know yet," Sherlock replied. "That woman didn't merely ask you to retrieve the map. She wanted to meet you and speak to you. She talked about your mother. She warned you not to tell anyone about that meeting. And then she disappeared into the cathedral. It's something much more complicated . . . almost as if she wanted to bring you to someone's attention."

"But why?" I asked. "I just got here, and I don't know anyone in Evreux!"

"Perhaps that's exactly why . . ."

The carriage, which Mr. Nelson was driving, slowed a bit.

Sherlock rubbed his knees with the palms of his hands and continued. "Or maybe it's because of the house you moved into. After all, it belonged to another nobleman from the *Almanac*, right?"

I stared down at the little red book I was holding on my lap. I was surprised that Sherlock had not only had time to browse through it, but that he even knew it so well.

"Whoa! Whoa!" Mr. Nelson called, pulling on the reins.

Sherlock headed out of the carriage. "Whatever the truth is, I hope we discover it here."

★ ★ ★

The Montmorency estate in Saint-Vigor was impressive. After the stables and a miniature temple at the entrance, a three-story house with a sloping roof came into view. The mansion was encircled by an Italian garden, split into geometric sections by walkways, large majolica vases, and white stone statues. The fountain, which should have been gushing between the two monumental staircases, had not yet been turned back on after the end of the cold season.

On the left side of the property, an English-style winter garden blossomed. There was a large glass pavilion, furnished with sofas and armchairs. As our carriage arrived, a large number of servants ran out to meet us.

Sherlock helped me out of the carriage. Escorted by my two friends and Mr. Nelson, who proceeded majestically behind us, I fearlessly walked up to the lean head of the Montmorency service.

"I'm Irene Adler d'Aurevilly," I introduced myself, trying to imitate my mother's haughty behavior that I had hated at other times. "And these are Misters Sherlock Winston Holmes . . . and Arsène DePuilles Lupin, of the DePuilles Lupins from Champagne."

I did not give him enough time to give more than the most minimal greeting, nor to try to place those thrown-together names with the ones he had already committed to memory as a servant of the house.

"I deeply regret having come here suddenly and unannounced," I continued, "but I must speak with Mr. Montmorency. And I must do so right away."

At that point, the butler's hands darted out in a well-practiced maneuver. "I'm very sorry, Miss Aurevilly."

"D'Aurevilly," Lupin broke in right away, to put the servant more on the spot.

"I meant, d'Aurevilly," he corrected himself. "But I'm afraid that Mr. Montmorency just —"

"Tell him that I have the map he's looking for with me," I interrupted.

The servant's hands waved around even more rapidly. "I don't believe it would be opportune. He just left . . . for Paris."

"I, however, have reason to believe it is very much opportune to try. We shall wait for him in the winter garden," I cut him short, trying not to blush or look down at my knees, which had grown weak.

"But of course," muttered the butler.

Our little procession headed to the glass pavilion. A maid opened the door, dressed in white and strutting like a goose. Lupin had her giggling with a silly remark, and we made ourselves at home on the edge of a sofa. Only then did I start to breathe again.

"How did I do?" I whispered.

"Just as your mother's been asking you to do for years," Mr. Nelson replied. "Regal and flawless."

Unsure whether to consider that an insult or a compliment, I remained silent. The sound of approaching steps made me prick up my ears.

"I'd say we're in," I murmured, gathering my friends together.

"I'd say not," Sherlock whispered.

And he was right, because the lean butler appeared a second time from the door leading into the mansion. "I'm terribly sorry, miss, but as I told you . . . Mr. Montmorency has just left for Paris. Therefore, it's absolutely impossible for you to speak to him."

"Yes, that is definitely a surprise," I commented, annoyed.

"So is the fact that poor Mr. d'Aurevilly had a daughter," he responded, raising an eyebrow. "Nevertheless, that's the way things are. Perhaps you and your friends have come all the way here for some other reason than what you've suggested . . ."

"To be precise," Lupin replied, crossing his arms, "Miss Irene Adler has recently moved into the d'Aurevilly house in Evreux, not far from here. And since then, in a lucky turn of events —"

"I believe I've found something that Mr. Montmorency is greatly interested in," I interrupted. I held back a sneeze, and then added, my heart in my throat, "But it could be that I'm incorrect."

"So the gentleman cannot receive us?" Sherlock insisted.

"Absolutely not." The butler stiffened.

I looked at my friends, trying to find a way to get out of this standoff and blew my nose. "You're telling me we came all this way for nothing?"

"I'm wondering if, by chance, you have it with you," the lean butler asked.

I looked for a handkerchief. Mr. Nelson handed one to me.

"Here with us? No. But we have every intention of negotiating with Mr. Montmorency," Arsène replied in my place. He pulled a white envelope out of his pocket, which bore an address written in a curlicued hand.

The butler looked at it sharply. "I believe Mr. Montmorency may be interested in reading what you propose," he replied stretching out his hand to take the envelope. "When he returns from Paris, I mean."

"Of course," Lupin echoed, pulling the envelope back from the butler with the speed of a kingfisher. He placed a hand on my shoulder.

"ACHOO!" I sneezed at that exact moment, burying my nose in Mr. Nelson's handkerchief. "Oh, good heavens!"

"I believe you've come down with a nasty cold, miss," the butler observed.

"And I fear that I will be needing a washroom as well," I added.

The butler straightened his spine and gestured to the maid strutting by. The last thing I saw before following her into the house was Lupin waving the white envelope like bait.

* * *

A few minutes later we were back in the carriage, heading out along the path from the Montmorencys' estate toward Saint-Vigor.

"What a horrible creature!" I remarked, flustered by the recent conversation with the Montmorency butler. "He was quite repulsive."

"But he wanted that envelope — and how," Arsène snickered. "I think we did well to have come all the way here."

The street to Saint-Vigor crossed through a thick grove. As soon as a lane opened to the side, Sherlock tapped on the coachman's box. Mr. Nelson reined in the horses, stopping the carriage.

"I think here would do well." Our friend thoughtfully nodded. As on the trip out, he had never stopped looking at the countryside surrounding us.

"What do you intend to do?" I asked.

As his only response, Sherlock opened up one of the suitcases and took out a change of clothes — a wool sweater, hunting pants, a heavy pair of boots — and began changing into them.

"I would say that it looks as though Master Holmes is about to go hunting," Mr. Nelson remarked from the coachman's box.

"Just so," Sherlock responded, hurriedly pulling off the elegant attire we had worn to present ourselves to the Montmorencys. "That butler wasn't honest with me, particularly since it looked to me like all the horses were in their stalls."

"And therefore, Mr. Montmorency was indeed at home," Arsène muttered, climbing down to the ground as well.

"But there's no need for you to get so worked up about it, Sherlock," I said.

"It won't take more than an hour," Holmes said. "I kept track of the distance to the house and cutting across from here —"

"You kept track of the distance, but I did better than that," Arsène interrupted, smiling. He pulled a small iron key out of his pocket. "You just need to smile at the servants who open the door . . ."

"Remarkable," Sherlock murmured. "But it wouldn't be a good idea to go in through the winter garden."

"Maybe you have a better idea?"

"Going behind the house," Sherlock replied.

"To enter where?"

"I don't know. But it's surer."

"Surer than a key?"

I looked at them, amazed. Was I wrong, or were those two fighting over who should go back to the estate and sneak in on Montmorency?

"Do you want to know which of you two wise guys is right?" I burst out, as Lupin and Sherlock went on standing up to each other.

They looked at me. They were acting like two roosters in a henhouse. I had to restrain myself from laughing.

"*I'm* right!" I said gleefully.

Mr. Nelson laid his gloves on his knees, prepared to enjoy what was to come.

"When I went to the washroom, I took advantage of the opportunity to leave the little back window ajar. If we hurry, we should find it's still open," I said.

"Miss!" Mr. Nelson broke in. "Even if I approved of your idea of sneaking into the house of a French nobleman like thieves, I don't think I'd risk *all* of you taking your chances and going adventuring."

"That's fine!" I said quickly. "If one of us —"

"Ahem!" Mr. Nelson coughed.

I huffed. Perhaps Mr. Nelson had become somewhat

of a partner in our adventures, but his presence still made me feel more limited than usual. "If one of you two . . . hurries," I said, "you should find it still open. But be careful."

"Well, I've almost finished changing," Sherlock announced.

"I'm already ready," Arsène retorted.

Sherlock held Lupin back with his arm. "We swore," he reminded him. "No tricks on each other."

"Odd," Arsène said, closing his fist.

"Even," Sherlock responded. He threw out a three with his fingers.

In the meantime, Arsène had thrown out a two. He won. He gave us a broad smile, a sarcastic bow, and disappeared into the forest.

★ ★ ★

We waited for Lupin at the little inn in Saint-Vigor. Sherlock tried to get rid of his long face and the feeling of defeat that was bothering him.

"I was sure I'd figured it out," he muttered after ordering a cup of tea.

"What?" I asked. "The odds and evens?"

He nodded. Scribbling a short mathematical formula on the table, he checked it and concluded. "With any opponent, saying 'even' and then throwing out an odd has a fifty-seven percent chance of winning. But with Arsène, who almost always plays three and five, my chances were almost eighty percent!"

"And the chances that sooner or later I am going to get angry with you are close to one hundred percent, Sherlock," I said.

He looked at me, still a little distant. Then he agreed that he did not need to puzzle over it so much. We drank our tea in silence, thinking over some of the topics of the last hour's discussion, unconcerned that anything bad would happen to Arsène.

When nearly forty minutes had passed, Sherlock and I walked around outside the inn to where Mr. Nelson was sitting in an iron chair, reading a little book by Mr. George Sand, which he seemed to be finding quite pleasant.

"Any news?" I asked.

"Perhaps the fact that this author signs his name as 'George,' but is actually a woman," Mr. Nelson commented, as if he wanted me to understand much more from his sentence.

We stepped away, and once we were out of Mr. Nelson's sight, Sherlock did something I had not expected.

"Wait," Holmes said. "There is something I'm forgetting . . ."

He pulled a golden pendant in the form of a heart from one of his pockets and put it in my hand, enjoying my stunned expression.

"How . . ."

Sherlock shrugged his shoulders. His long, sharp nose reddened. "Yesterday, in the barn, I spotted it on the ground and thought it would give you pleasure to have it back."

I squeezed it in my palm. "Yes, definitely." I wavered, but then I found the courage I needed to ask him, "Sherlock, in view of the oath we swore . . ."

He waited, staring at me.

"Could you tell if it was you who gave it to me?"

He smiled. "If I answer you, will you give me your word that you won't ask me that again?"

I nodded.

So did he.

"Yes," he replied, pointing to the pendant. "I just gave it to you. Is it the same one?"

And so I understood that even the oaths we'd sworn had their dark side. And that when I asked questions or answered them, I needed to think very carefully about what to say — especially when dealing with Sherlock Holmes.

★ ★ ★

Lupin arrived at the inn two hours later, literally covered in mud and coated with something better not specified, much darker and more foul smelling. Its stench quickly filled the entire inside of the carriage as we departed. Despite his appearance and the smell, he was beaming.

"I discovered two things," he announced. "Actually, three."

From his position in the coachman box, Mr. Nelson asked Lupin to speak louder, as he could not hear him very well.

"The first," Lupin continued, "is that they have a huge pigsty at the Montmorency mansion."

Sherlock burst out laughing. So did I. That was where that stench had come from!

"I had to hide there for almost an hour," Lupin confessed. "But it was worth it. My friends, this is something really big. Much more important than any of the others we've been involved in up until now. We're talking about . . . high nobility. I don't know if you understand what I mean."

"Go on," Sherlock said.

"Don't keep us in suspense, Arsène," I added.

"Mr. Montmorency had absolutely not left, as the butler led us to believe, but was hiding on the estate, exactly as Sherlock supposed."

"Clearly," Holmes commented.

"As soon as I went into the house through the little window in the washroom," Lupin continued, "I saw him conversing with his butler. They were talking about that Bernache —"

"That scoundrel who sent his stooges to rob me," I said.

"Exactly," Lupin continued. "They agreed that it had been a very poor choice. And that they would need to change methods as soon as possible . . . or else they would not get the map."

"Did they read our message?" I asked.

"You bet! It must have been the first thing they did, because they were very excited. They were all convinced we had decided to negotiate to sell our fragment of the map. Because you were right about this, too, Sherlock: that parchment is part of a map."

Our friend Sherlock stifled an expression of visible satisfaction behind his habitually composed mask.

"But there's one thing that even you couldn't know. Actually, two things," Arsène said. "The first is that there is someone else behind Mr. Montmorency. A person they call the Grand Master. And he's the one who gave the orders to retrieve the fragments of the map."

"The Grand Master . . ." I murmured. Those words stuck in my head as if in a spider's web.

"So Bernache had to find the part of the map that Montmorency was supposed to deliver to this . . . Grand Master," Sherlock said. "And you discovered his name and where he lives?"

"No, no name," Lupin said. "But I figured out that he communicates with them via mysterious messages. Which all come from Paris, naturally."

"Paris!" Sherlock exclaimed. "I suspected that."

"But that's not all," Arsène continued. "Montmorency himself possesses a fragment of the map that's very similar to Irene's."

"You saw it?"

Arsène got a sly expression on his face. "I did a little something more, really," he murmured.

"So perhaps we should say that Montmorency *used* to possess a fragment of the map?" Sherlock asked with an amused smile.

"And that he lost it in the pigsty?" I added.

"Exactly," that rascal Arsène Lupin answered, pulling the fragment of the map out from his filthy clothes.

Chapter 11

A JOINT DECISION

Once again, the three of us — Sherlock, Lupin, and I — found ourselves in the attic of the d'Aurevilly house by candlelight. A steady drizzle beat against the windows. From time to time, one of the nearby branches scratched noisily against the roof.

Kneeling on the ground, Sherlock was trying to match up the two fragments of the map as Lupin and I looked on. After a couple of attempts, he arranged them one above the other along the left side of a bigger, invisible square.

"They're from the same map," he decided after looking at them carefully.

I only saw lines with illegible, faded handwriting, except one line that was thicker than the others. It looked like a snake or a branch, or something twisty. Apart from that, they were just yellowed parchments smelling strongly of dust.

"A map of what?" I asked.

"Of the city of Paris," said Sherlock, without thinking twice.

I could not figure out how Holmes had come to that conclusion, and it seemed to me that even Lupin was at a loss. But we were both in awe of our friend's confidence.

Sherlock pointed a finger at a line that was drawn heavier than the others. "This is the Seine, the river in Paris," he explained. "It traces precisely this bend as it leaves the city."

I stayed silent, looking at the map.

"Of course," Lupin commented.

"You can check if you want," Sherlock added.

Wrapped in his bathrobe, Lupin sat down on the floor. Despite the hot bath that Mr. Nelson had arranged for him on the ground floor in the back of the house, Lupin still smelled of the pigsty, and I imagined that he probably would for days.

"I believe you, I believe you," he blurted out. "So now we have two fragments of an old map of Paris . . . what do we do with them?"

"In order to answer you, my friend, I should need to see all of it, with the eight pieces that form it," Sherlock said.

"Or ask Mr. Montmorency," I said.

"I doubt he knows," Holmes replied. "Rather, it would be better to ask the Grand Master of Paris."

A map of Paris. The Grand Master of Paris. All the clues were telling us we should go to the capital if we wanted to unravel this mystery.

"But what does all this have to do with my mother?" I asked. "And the lady in the cathedral?"

Neither of them could answer that.

"The facts are more straightforward than we think," Sherlock pontificated at that point. And as so often happened to him in those moments of self-pride, he grew silent.

"And that would be, if you please?" Arsène asked him.

"I believe you should try to talk to your mother, Irene, and discover what she knows about this story, without telling her anything about the map."

I nodded. It seemed necessary at that point, even if in my heart, I felt it would be better never to tackle that discussion with her. "I can do it tomorrow afternoon, when I go to read *Paul and Virginia* to her. Then, that evening —"

"Wait. Wait. Another fact, Arsène, is that you can't keep hiding yourself away in this attic," our English friend interrupted. "Sooner or later you have to go back to your father."

"You can forget about that!" Lupin retorted.

But Holmes ignored him. "In the meantime," he continued, "my week of freedom in Brussels will soon come to an end. My friends, the facts tell us that if we really want to solve this mystery, we must split up and then get back together quickly, no more than two days from this evening, to tell each other what we've discovered."

"Sherlock, what are you saying? We've just found each other again!" I tried to object. But it was useless.

"Arsène, you and I need to leave tomorrow morning as early as possible to look for this Grand Master in Paris, while you, Irene, will talk with your mother to find out what she really knows," Sherlock said. He rummaged through his pockets, pulling out a meager roll of banknotes. "I should still have enough francs to pay for a couple of nights out . . . if you don't want to rely on your father."

"I'd rather sleep in the street!" Lupin declared.

"But I would not," Sherlock responded. "Plus I have a suitcase to take back to London. And I have time until I have to return the day after tomorrow. Give me the name of a hotel you know."

"Why? There are thousands of them," Lupin replied, shrugging.

Sherlock insisted until Arsène decided they would stay at the Alchemists, a dive in the IX arrondissement. That night my anxious young spirit was confronted by thousands of doubts. I decided to try to dissuade my friends from the idea of going to the capital.

"Papa says that every kind of danger lurks there," I said. "There are soldiers patrolling every street . . . starving, poor people roam the neighborhoods . . . and there are fires."

But they were adamant, just as they were also adamant about my staying at Evreux, where I should wait for their letter or, as Arsène said many times, his return.

And so they left.

★ ★ ★

When I got up for breakfast the next morning, I was alone. My father had left at sunrise to take care of some business in the city of Amiens.

Mr. Nelson greeted me warmly. He confirmed that my guest, Sherlock Holmes, had left in a carriage at the crack of dawn.

"Alone?" I asked him.

Without waiting for a reply, I ran up to the attic. But I found it deserted.

I slipped my hand under my collar and squeezed the golden pendant that Sherlock had given me (possibly twice), feeling only a sad distance.

Mr. Nelson hovered around me that morning, trying to tell me a secret. When I finally let him do so, he told me that Masters Holmes and Lupin had left the two fragments of the map in his custody and that they only had a copy with them, which Master Holmes had sketched out with great precision.

Evidently, Sherlock Holmes had not slept the previous night.

I withdrew into a beastly silence, which I did not even break at lunch, despite Mr. Nelson's attempts to temper my bad mood.

In the afternoon, I went to Mama's room at the usual time. I found her sitting on her little sofa, smiling. I don't know why, but her smile seemed to reject me, almost hatefully.

I had difficulty reading, and Mama noticed it.

"Is everything all right, Irene?" she asked.

"No, everything is not all right," I would've liked to have answered.

Nothing was all right at all, because a mysterious woman had involved me in a shady affair that I could not understand, and my two true friends had left at dawn to help me solve it.

I felt overwhelmed by a totally groundless, terrible rage. Closing the book with bad grace, I let it fall to the ground.

"Irene?"

I looked up at her. "Mama?" I asked. "Do you know anything about a certain map of Paris? A map divided into eight parts?"

Her expression turned both stunned and frightened. "What are you talking about?"

"Did you ever know a blond woman . . . someone who you talked to about me . . . and who is looking for a map of Paris?"

I saw her try to get to her feet, her legs trembling beneath her. "Irene, I don't understand what . . . you're talking about —"

"What about Mr. d'Aurevilly? Did you know him? And the Montmorencys? Do you know any of them?" I went on.

"No, Irene, no! But why are you asking me these questions? And why are you being so . . . aggressive?" my mother asked.

"Then why do they know me, Mama?" I persisted, wanting an answer.

Mama flopped onto the little sofa. She leaned her head against one of the columns that held up the canopy and whispered with her last bit of strength, "Irene, what on earth has come over you?"

I left the room in a rage, my blood boiling. I went and shut myself up in my room. I heard Mr. Nelson's footsteps and my mother's agitated voice, and that was enough for me.

That evening, when our butler knocked on the door to my lilac-colored room to invite me to come down for dinner, he found it empty, with two dresses fewer in the wardrobe.

He realized immediately that I had escaped via the steps hidden in the vines. But it took him almost a day to realize that Arsène Lupin's boneshaker had disappeared from the garden.

I was a day ahead of him, and I was raised in Paris. Once I got there, I would have no difficulty finding the Alchemists Hotel.

Chapter 12

THE ALCHEMISTS
OF PARIS

The term *boneshaker*, I decided, was not just a nickname, but also the true name of that diabolical wheeled device.

When I could finally glimpse the walls of Paris, it was a little past noon, and I no longer could feel my back, let alone my backside. I located a postal stop from its sign, went into a small inn, and, francs in hand, asked for a ride. It felt like a luxurious way to travel, seated next to the postal worker on a hard carriage box. I imagined Arsène's expression when I told him where I had left his iron contraption.

Believe me, after that trip I was absolutely certain that no one would ever be able to invent a comfortable bicycle, let alone that anyone who was not as crazy as Arsène would ever be able to ride one.

After the long siege of that winter and the resulting starvation, Paris had turned gray. The streets were mostly deserted — few people, few inns open, and no animals running loose, as had been the case in the past. The famine must have been even more terrible than I had supposed. The Luxembourg Gardens seemed covered with ashes, which shocked me, as did the string of closed, barred windows along Napoleon's residences.

I thanked the postal worker for giving me a ride and set about looking for the Alchemists Hotel, heading toward the quarter where they had told me it was located — the *Marais*. Not so long ago, the *Marais* had been a swamp, and now it was a maze of short houses and narrow alleys. I found the Alchemists just before the *rue du Temple*, where the money changers' and pawnbrokers' shops began. There, embarrassed Parisians handed over their most valuable goods in exchange for a handful of francs. *Papa was right*, I thought, as I passed a grimy, wet intersection. For some people, war was an opportunity. Every event and every action that man took caused unexpected consequences, upward or downward. Someone is always higher than us, and someone is always lower than us.

Above, I noticed that the trees seemed unconcerned about the fate of the war, for the first buds and tender leaflets were already sprouting. Below, strong, revolting smells seeped out through the half-open doors. Cabbage soup in the best circumstances. Mouse, shoe, and belt soup when there was nothing else. As always, poverty and luxury were no more than a few blocks apart, but in entirely different worlds.

Sherlock and Lupin were not in their room, but the woman who ran the little hotel knew exactly who I was inquiring about. When I asked her if she had a room for me, she scrutinized me coldly, as if she was guessing my age and the amount of francs I had with me.

She said she did not. *In order to negotiate over the price,* I thought.

I did not want her to realize how confused and frightened I was. I kept thinking that I had run away from home and was completely alone in a city that had just emerged from a war. But to the eyes of outsiders, I wanted to show myself to be a worldly, independent girl. I could not know how ridiculous this must have seemed.

"If you really want," the woman suggested, "I can have a straw pallet added to your friends' room."

My eyes lit up. "That would be perfect!" I exclaimed.

"But it will still cost you as much as a single room for yourself," she clarified.

That was fine with me. My first concern was not about money, but about finding myself in Paris without any plan.

I asked her where I could get a bite to eat, and the woman peered at me again, her expression like that of a wolf. "It depends how much you want to spend, miss."

"It doesn't matter," I replied. "I'll take care of it myself."

I found myself on one of the bridges that crossed the Seine, not far from *l'Île de La Cité* and the black spires of Notre-Dame. The river flowed slowly, carrying debris with it.

I wandered near the *Lutèce* arena, to the one building I knew well — my home. It broke my heart to see the windows and front door barred. What been the window of my bedroom overlooked a small park, where boards, planks, and rubble were thrown together now. Only two of the trees surrounding the fountain had survived the chaos.

A woman walking near the walls looked like one of our maids, and I thought of calling out to her. But I stopped myself, putting a hand over my mouth. I was not sure it was her, and I realized that even if it had been, I would not have known what to say.

So I went back to the hotel, reaching it at the end of the afternoon. A glance from the woman on the ground floor was all I needed to know that Lupin and Sherlock had returned.

I climbed the wooden stairs of that filthy dump two by two, knocked on the door, and cried, "Lupin! Sherlock!"

"Irene!" Arsène hopped up. "So that old crone wasn't having us on. It's really you!"

"In flesh and blood, gentlemen, despite your shake-everything vehicle!" I said.

"You must be crazy!" Sherlock greeted me. "Coming all the way here alone."

"And how are you so sure I was alone?"

"From seeing how you're dressed, I'd say," Sherlock said, raising an eyebrow. "And because the woman downstairs told us we should go down to the cellar and get a third pallet to put in the room."

It was useless to pretend. In a few words, I told them of my flight from home. It seemed an adventure worthy of Rocambole, the gentleman thief I'd read three books about, written by the Viscount Ponson du Terrail.

"What about you?" I asked.

"We need a hearty dinner!" Lupin roared.

"Or at least the Parisian equivalent," Sherlock added.

I snorted and asked, "Is eating the only thing you know how to do?"

"Whether you believe it or not, Irene, a hearty meal may be the only way to figure out more about the Grand Master."

Sherlock explained to me that thanks to his brother Mycroft and his subscription to *The World Literary Gazette* (a showy periodical filled with information about the latest literary news), Sherlock had found a clue about the Grand Master.

"And how can that help us?" I asked, puzzled.

"Simple! I remembered that the article in question spoke of a Parisian writer . . . Mr. Alexandre Dumas!"

Hearing the name of the author of *The Three Musketeers* greatly surprised me.

"Alexandre Dumas?" I stammered. "You mean *that* Alexandre Dumas? He's still alive?"

"Unfortunately not. He died last December," Sherlock replied. "But his son, who has the same name, is still alive. Although he's not the writer his father was, in my opinion, he might be able to help us. The two worked hand in glove with each other!"

"Oh, and where —" I began.

"I made a little visit to the French Academy!" Lupin interrupted with a clever smile. "A peek at their address book was enough to find out where our Dumas lives."

"And a chat with his very friendly maid yielded his habits," Sherlock added.

According to what Dumas's housekeeper said, the writer usually dined at Francillon, an expensive restaurant that had somehow managed to keep up its business, despite the war.

We headed to the restaurant, which was near the big church of *Saint-Eustache*, located inside the borders of the park of *Les Halles*.

Lupin reached the revolving door and pushed it. The aroma of roasted meat, game, and baked potatoes enveloped us.

We asked for Dumas *fils*. Lupin was doing the asking, and since he'd retained an excellent accent, despite his roaming, he received the answer, "Of course!"

We followed the waiter to a small table in the corner, where a fancy gentleman with luxurious, gelled hair and a prominent chin sat. He had a large stained napkin stretched across his chest.

"Mr. Dumas?" Lupin began. "Please forgive me for disturbing you."

The diner barely raised his eyes from the wine that was being poured, immediately assuming a suspicious expression.

"I hope you haven't come to ask me about my father's books," he began drily when he saw three children standing before him.

"Absolutely not," Lupin hastened to respond. "On the contrary, I must confess we've never read them."

I wanted to object that I had devoured *The Count of Montecristo* and *The Three Musketeers*, but I thought it better to support Arsène's game. And sure enough, his claim had somewhat of an effect.

"So what do you want?" Dumas asked. "I don't think you want a meal, I imagine, nor do you seem old enough to invite me to accept a post in the socialist government . . . although you never know, when officials spend their time shrieking, 'Power to the young!' And so, as I already said, I'm not interested."

Sherlock seemed annoyed by this rant, but limited himself to a look of disapproval. I, however, noticed

Dumas glancing over at me as he spoke, as if he hoped I would at least laugh a little. He looked back and forth between us, his head bobbing like a ship in the middle of the sea. So I smiled.

"None of those, actually," my friend continued. "Allow me to introduce myself. My name is Arsène Lupin, artist and juggler."

"Oh, good grief," Alexandre Dumas muttered under his breath.

"And with me are Master Sherlock Holmes, puzzle buff, and Miss Irene Adler . . . writer."

I snapped a fiery glance at him. Why had he introduced me that way?

"Oh, really?" Dumas chuckled, looking at me a little more carefully. "A writer? And what do you write?"

"Murder mysteries," I replied, without hesitation.

He seemed to leap out of his chair. "A delicate young lady like you writes murder mysteries? What kind?"

"All kinds of them," I replied. "I don't have a preference. As long as someone dies." I looked at Lupin. "And someone investigates." I looked at Sherlock.

"I don't believe it!" Dumas exclaimed, greatly amused. "I'll have to introduce you to my friend, George!" Then he arranged his napkin around the collar of his shirt and grabbed his silverware, because his pigs' feet and potatoes had arrived. They had an aroma good enough to twist a hungry stomach into knots. "But the fact remains that I still don't know why you —"

"We're looking for the Grand Master," Sherlock interrupted from behind Lupin and me. And we've been told you might know who he is."

At those words, Alexandre Dumas set down his fork, and his face turned ashen. After a moment of church-like silence, he displayed a forced smile. "The Grand Master, eh?"

"Precisely."

"And you say you've never read my father's books?"

"I actually have," I admitted. "But as I recall, they don't speak of a Grand Master."

He asked what I might have read, and hearing my reply, he murmured, "Oh, of course, of course. Those are probably my papa's best novels. Even though, you know, it wasn't really he who wrote them, or at least not entirely. So you've never read any of the novels from the series about Marie Antoinette . . ."

I shook my head.

"Not even *Joseph Balsamo, the Count of Cagliostro?*"

Once again, I gestured no.

"However," Sherlock Holmes broke in, "we know that your father was working on a last, great work . . . And I believe we must find out something about it."

The man started and gave my friend an anxious look, forgetting the plate before him for a moment. "And you," he asked in a whisper. "What do you know about that work?"

Chapter 13

THE DUMAS ARCHIVES

When I remember our adventure, even today, I am astonished that in the end, three children like us — who had just arrived in Paris without even having an address to look for — were able to convince a man to take us to his home and tell us about his family's secrets. The fact is that my friend, Sherlock Holmes, was convincing. Having consumed his pig's feet, Alexandre Dumas *fils* put on his coat and made his way to the *rue Coquillière*, where we could still smell a neighborhood market, continuing onward to the intersection with the *rue Croix des Petits Champs*, where we curved toward *rue Saint-Honoré*.

"Not everything my father wrote was true," Dumas confided, as we walked through the city, ticking along with his walking stick. "And believing his words would be like betting on a blindfolded horse. But I think the Grand Master was something entirely different for once. Papa was a genuine fan of mysterious things and people. Of what you children call the 'supernatural.'"

We followed Alexandre Dumas *fils* up to a doorway, where he pulled out his keys and opened the door on the third try. "My father had a strong point," he said. "Before writing about something, he gathered information on it. And he kept everything he'd found, cataloging it and filing it away."

We went up a flight of stairs and then a second one. Alexandre Dumas *fils* spoke without pausing; not even Arsène could stem the flow. When we reached a door, he stopped to look at us in the dark. For a moment, I was afraid we'd been too naïve by following him there.

"What I know about my father's final, terrible, unfinished book is that it's based on a true story that he collected information about. Apparently, despite being protected by the deepest secrecy, the Grand Master holds the fate of the city in his hands — and, without exaggerating, the fate of all of France. They call him the Grand Master of the Order of St. Michael, and he is said to meet with his followers in the tunnels under Paris in order to carry out secret rites and horrific rituals . . . intended to restore the old regime of France!"

Saying this, Alexandre Dumas *fils* flung open the door to an apartment. It was almost completely empty, except for two rows of writing tables on which a few menacing wood and metal machines were lined up. They attracted our attention right away.

"Welcome to what the family, if one can speak of family, calls the haunted chamber. These are six Ravizza writing keyboards, originally from Italy," he explained, showing the first models of what — over the course of years I would learn to call a "typewriter," which ended up having such significance in my life.

He touched them lightly with his fingertips, passing across them. "My father loved inventions and spending money in the most eccentric ways."

"It's like being in a newsroom," Sherlock observed.

"Here's where he created some of his most famous works — he and his assistants, the ghosts who worked with him. Which includes yours truly, of course."

So saying, Dumas lit a light and, holding it high above his head, moved into a second room. It was occupied by an enormous chest of drawers manufactured out of good, sturdy wood that held the Dumas Archives.

There were no labels, only drawers. Drawers and more drawers, one after another. Newspapers were thrown in a messy pile on the floor, plus books. Books by both Dumas men.

Before finding what he was looking for, Dumas opened and closed a few drawers, all of which were filled to the brim with pages from newspapers, handwritten notes, pictures, and stamps. When he finally caught sight of the bundle he'd been looking for, he grabbed it. A loose sheet fluttered out and fell to the ground. Sherlock, who was nearest, promptly bent down to pick it up and handed it to the writer, who stuck it in his pocket.

"Make yourselves at home," he said.

We arranged ourselves on the carpet. He began running some notes through his fingers, mumbling. Whenever he found an interesting one, he read it aloud. "The Grand Master and the map of Paris . . . could it be this?"

It seemed to fit. It was just a reference to the existence of a map (we hadn't admitted to having two fragments of it with us), which convinced Dumas to bring it over to us.

"So, ladies and gentlemen," Dumas said, "it appears

that the person who suggested you speak to me did you a great service."

"So it seems," Lupin admitted.

"What does your note say?" Sherlock inquired.

"I'd advise you not to speak to anyone about these matters, on pain of death. You're just children, but I think you can understand that you are faced with something much bigger than you are. It says here that the power of the Grand Master comes from a map . . . A map that shows the place where the holiest of relics is preserved in the vaults of Paris, a place known as the Heart of St. Michael."

Alexandre Dumas *fils* looked at us, horrified. "A relic of immense power, capable of curing all evil, present and past, and restoring the order of things as they should be, or something like that."

"And apparently there are people prepared to do anything to get this map," I reflected.

"Oh, no doubt about it, miss! Whoever has this relic in their possession, especially in a difficult time like this, can certainly —"

"Does your note say anything else?" interrupted Sherlock, who had little tolerance for what he undoubtedly thought were silly fantasies.

"Oh, yes, it does. Papa drew this design." He showed us a pencil sketch that depicted France, roughly. A few cities were shown on it, connected by a dotted line.

After studying it, Sherlock remarked, "The constellation Virgo . . ."

"Exactly!" Dumas explained. "The French Gothic cathedrals are located through France so as to duplicate that constellation."

"A detail worthy of a novel!" Lupin commented, amused.

The writer gave him a dirty look. "My father drew a few lines on this sheet, with tiny writing on it. The map was divided between eight ancient noble French families, who were to protect it until . . ."

"Until?" I asked.

"I'm sorry," he said. "The sentence breaks off there. And we can no longer ask him what he had in mind."

Eight families, I thought, and I looked at the drawing that the son of the great writer was holding out to me. Evreux had one of the cathedrals depicted. An ancient pact to hide a relic of great importance, an object for recovery during tumultuous times, like those we were passing through. Eight families and eight pieces of a map, as Sherlock Holmes had already guessed.

It was enough to begin to understand more about the mystery, but we still were missing essential clues.

"Your father doesn't say who the Grand Master is or how to go about finding him?" I asked.

"Oh, no. That he doesn't say," Dumas replied.

"And do we have a list of the eight families?"

"Not even that, unfortunately."

"So we find ourselves at a . . . dead end?"

"Actually, young lady, we're in an apartment filled with dusty, old notes and ghosts of ghosts, if you'll permit me to play with words. A dead end is only a problem if you want to proceed along a certain road at any cost . . . But I have no intention of following my father's clues about this fearsome story," Alexandre Dumas *fils* concluded, retrieving his father's note.

Chapter 14

THE LADY OF
THE CAMELLIAS

Sherlock, Lupin, and I all slept heavily, without changing our clothes, due to the conditions of the sheets and the many tiny inhabitants of our filthy little room. Since my two friends politely let me choose, I took the most isolated pallet in the room and immediately regretted it.

In the deep silence of the Parisian night, it was a great comfort to hear Lupin and Sherlock breathing. Lupin tossed and turned frequently under his filthy covers as if he was having trouble getting to sleep, while Sherlock's breath was regular and measured. He lay motionless on his pallet, like a motor that was off but ready to turn back on again at the slightest signal.

For instance, a distant explosion awakened me during the night, causing me to jump from my bed. Lupin swore, without really awakening, while Sherlock had sprung to his feet and was already looking out the tiny window when I sat up.

It's nothing, I told myself. *Maybe a weapons depot. Maybe a collapsing house.* But my heart beat wildly, and Sherlock looked at me in the dark.

Without saying a word, we pushed my pallet closer to his. When we fell back asleep again, we were much closer to each other, and I felt better protected.

★ ★ ★

We woke early. Still wavering between day and night, the Paris sky was a dark blue mixed with the gray of dawn. It seemed to me that the first light of that day brought a promise with it. The promise of events that would soon take place.

While I got ready, trying to look presentable, a thought kept coming back to sting me like a barb. I thought about how much I must have worried my parents, leaving home as I had. I worried over how to let them know in a way that wouldn't force me to give up our adventure.

In the end, I gave up on the idea with a sigh. Was it really only the adventure of three daring children? Or was it, instead, an opportunity — perhaps the only one — to discover something important about my family? Indeed, the answer would come shortly afterward in the form of a life-changing revelation.

As soon as we were able to find an open café, we sat down at a table. We sipped a blackish concoction and ate a chunk of stale bread. But it was warm, which seemed wonderful to me.

Sherlock did not even look at the breakfast we had been served. Motionless and angular, his profile stood out against the café window.

"If this were a game of chess, it would be our turn to make a move now," he suddenly said. "Any suggestions?"

His question caught me by surprise, and — still shrouded in a sleepy haze — I tried to collect my thoughts. All I could do was feel amazed when I thought of all my friends and I had just done.

My flight to Paris to follow the trail of a mysterious person who had somehow directed the actions of other, equally mysterious figures (the woman from the cathedral, Mr. Montmorency, and his useless pawns) now stood out in all its absurdity. And the conversation with

Alexandre Dumas *fils* did nothing past making everything even more incredible. For a moment I felt as if I had been swallowed up by a serialized story.

"Maybe that woman I met in front of the Evreux cathedral was nothing more than a madwoman!" I said, thinking it all over.

But Sherlock shook his head. "And Montmorency? And his thugs? It would have to be a true epidemic of madness, don't you think?"

My friend was right, but his question fell on deaf ears. Lupin was unresponsive, as if he was having trouble shaking off the weight of a bad dream he'd had the previous night.

I saw him grab his cup with an almost angry gesture. In a single gulp, he drank the whole blackish swill that they passed off as coffee.

"Listen," Lupin then said, with the air of someone who had just made a decision. "There's only one thing we can do, even though it will be . . . far from pleasant for me."

Neither Sherlock nor even I could have guessed what Arsène was about to propose. We listened without saying a word as he reeled off the story of his family as we had never heard it. From the dark circles under his eyes and the way he wrung his hands as he spoke, I realized this decision had kept him awake all night.

In a few very dry words, and without ever ceasing to look right at us, Lupin told us who his mother was — a French noblewoman named Marie de Vaudron-Chantal, who had rebelled against her family by going out with Theophraste Lupin. It is not known — nor could Arsène tell us — whether theirs had been a short, genuine love affair or a mere act of rebellion. The fact is that the romantic tale between a rich noblewoman and a man of the streets had not worked out, and the couple had not been able to withstand societal pressure. So they had separated, in a cold but civilized way, as if the fading of that impossible passion had stretched a curtain of ice between their ways of seeing the world.

Arsène had grown up on the road with his father and the other circus artists. And despite his father's attempts to keep this from being the case, Arsène had developed a sense of disdain toward his mother, fed, more than anything else, by his profound awareness that she had abandoned him.

"All that matters now is that my mother lives near here . . . and I think she could tell us something useful," Lupin concluded.

"And are you willing to —" I began.

"Only if you come with me," he replied, lowering his gaze.

Back then, I simply understood Lupin's request instinctively.

But today, writing so many years later, I understand its deeper meaning: one cannot face the most terrible solitudes alone.

★ ★ ★

The Vaudron-Chantal mansion was white, with all its shutters open. There was something impolite about how clean the building was, as if it were a challenge to all that was happening in the rest of the city. We reached it after a long walk uphill — even that detail contributed to the mansion's extravagant, haughty atmosphere.

Lupin announced himself at what seemed to be a porter's lodge. In turn, a man who was in charge of the gate led us to a perfectly circular inner courtyard, so pretty that it resembled a tart from a *patisserie*.

Neither Sherlock nor I spoke much, respecting the difficulties Lupin was coping with to carry out our investigation.

"Actually, this has never been my home," he revealed to us as the porter disappeared into the corridor of the mansion. "I remember very little about this place. A Christmas party, snow, a large parlor. Little else." At that point, he let the conversation die.

"Last Christmas, which we spent together, was much better," he continued, with a forced smile. "Risking life and limb on the Thames River!"

I smiled, patting his hand. Every second of waiting seemed as if it were a further insult, as if the hostile environment wanted to make him finally understand that he was an outsider.

When the porter finally returned, he led us, without apology, down a hallway and a narrow staircase intended for the servants — which they could use to reach different floors of the house without being noticed. My feeling of discomfort grew even more severe. Neither Arsène nor the company he had brought was deemed worthy of the mansion's main staircase.

So I was surprised that we were received in a library, a vast room above the rooftops of Paris. Its walls were filled with gilded publications and that sense of clutter that shows someone really uses it and that it is, therefore, not merely a collection of valuable books. On a table in the middle of the room, a bunch of white camellias gave off their intense, sweet perfume.

"Arsène," a very beautiful woman greeted him as soon as the service door opened ahead of us.

I was dazzled. So, too, was Sherlock, I am sure.

Our friend Arsène's mother was a gorgeous woman. Taller than the norm, lean and slender with long, full black hair and blue eyes like those of a Siamese cat. Her face was a long, perfect oval, and her eyebrows were arched, which seemed to emphasize the meaning of her words.

And yet, from the way she approached her son and avoided embracing him, I understood Lupin's discomfort. That gorgeous woman was distant. Absent. Cold.

"Madame Vaudron-Chantal," he greeted her, his voice hesitant. He moved about the library, more awkward than I had ever seen him, without even looking around. "It's a pleasure to see you."

"A completely unexpected surprise. What —"

"I would like to introduce my two dearest friends to you," Lupin continued, pointing us out to his mother. "Irene Adler and Sherlock Holmes."

The lady greeted us with the perfect manners of a Parisian aristocrat.

"It's a real honor meet you," I said, curtsying. "Arsène has told us much about you."

She could not hold back a smile. "About me? Really? He speaks more of me with you than of you with me, then. How many years has it been since you've answered my letters, Arsène? I've lost count by now. And where are you living at the moment? What are you doing? Perhaps your friends can help me discover who and what my son has become?"

"We're not here for this," Lupin said drily, letting his gaze roam along the long rows of books and paintings on the shelves.

"So why, then? Is there a specific reason? Maybe your father . . ."

"My father's not involved in this," Lupin said. "There's a reason, but it doesn't concern me, nor them, nor my life."

I felt like I was attending more than a meeting between mother and son, but rather a match in some terrible game whose rules only the two of them knew. And which it seemed of vital importance to win.

"So why, then, have you come back?"

"For the simplest of reasons. I need help. We need help."

"Oh," said Madame Vaudron-Chantal, going over to a table with small drawers made of inlaid wood.

"The help I'm looking for is the answer to a simple question."

"My goodness! I see my son again for the first time in five years and all he can say to me is that he wants the answer to a simple question!" Arsène's mother smiled at me — I don't know why — and then continued. "Have you ever wondered, all this time, how many replies I would have liked, myself? From you or your father? Can you add up the infinite number of questions I've had about you both? Are they all right? Are they cold? Are they eating enough? Is Arsène really studying, as Theophraste assured me he would before disappearing again? Will I be able to recognize my son? Why don't they respond to any of my letters? Did they ever receive them? Do they actually exist? Or are they just a figment of my imagination?"

Lupin did not reply, but his face grew hard and sharp like the blade of a knife. He tried to speak, but his mother spoke first.

"Now you listen here," she said in a firm tone. "And the two of you will forgive me if this conversation takes place in your presence and not in private, as it should. But if you really are his two best friends, then I prefer there be witnesses to what I'm about to say."

"Mama . . ." Arsène whispered weakly.

"We are, ma'am," Sherlock broke in. "Even though it's true we've only known each other less than a year, and it's not my habit to speak for others, I can confirm that your son's introduction was correct."

"A boy who can speak!" the lady exclaimed.

"Mama . . ." Lupin tried once again to step in. But he was like a runner wheezing from exhaustion.

"My proposal is the following, Arsène. I give you the help you're looking for — as much as I can, I mean. But in exchange, you and I must speak. You must promise to come here, alone, to this house. And to tell me everything."

Lupin raised his eyes to the ceiling.

"I want a week," his mother continued. "You owe it to me. A week — not a day more nor a day less."

Silence fell in the library. It seemed to last forever.

"Can you promise me this?" she finally asked.

We waited.

"Yes," Arsène whispered.

"What did you say?"

"I said, 'yes.'"

She took a deep breath and seemed to grow smaller. I had judged her wrongly. Beyond her icy, upper-class demeanor was a mother who was worried about her son. And this meeting had been no less exhausting for her than for Arsène.

"So," she said, leaning back in her chair. "What do you want to ask me?"

Lupin looked at me, as if he no longer had the strength to talk.

"What Arsène wants to ask you, ma'am," I began, "is if you know the d'Aurevilly family."

"I know them like everyone else," she replied calmly, "but not personally."

"And the Montmorencys?" I asked.

"I am obliged to answer you in the same way, young lady. I believe I have visited them once or maybe twice. But not regularly, if what you need is an introduction to society. I don't like that kind of life."

"And have you ever heard talk of the Grand Master?" I went on.

The woman's long eyebrows furrowed then. After a long moment of silence, she turned to her son and asked in a quiet voice, "Arsène, what business have you gotten yourself into?"

"No business, Mama, but —" he murmured.

"You don't plan to tell me about it?" she interreupted.

Then Madame Vaudron-Chantal turned to me. "So then what is this story about the Grand Master?"

"I know it's hard to believe, but we don't exactly know," I admitted. "What would help . . . is to find the person who is known as the Grand Master."

"And my son convinced you I could help you find him?" she asked.

We both looked at Lupin, who looked at his mother. "I'm sure you know something," he muttered.

"That's an absolutely absurd idea, Arsène!" she exclaimed.

"Mama . . . you promised."

Lupin's mother sighed deeply. "I promised. And you promised, too. A week?"

"A week," Lupin replied.

Madame Vaudron-Chantal invited us to be seated in the library armchairs and told us what she knew.

They were no more than voices, perhaps little more than whispers and information repeated through the mansions of the Parisian nobility, who had been gripped these past months by harrowing uncertainty. I had the strange feeling that with these words, Arsène's mother was echoing the old stories that Mr. Dumas *père* had unearthed for his unfinished novel. According to the legend, a few noble families in the city were guardians of a secret that would let them restore the old regime and put the aristocracy and clergy in charge of France again. Madame Vaudron-Chantal also told us about a relic hidden in a crypt in the depths of Paris, and of a sacred ritual that was supposed to release enormous supernatural power.

"Opinions are extremely vague as to what those powers might exactly be," Lupin's mother concluded, her hands fluttering about.

The story that Lupin's mother told only lasted a few minutes, but when we said goodbye and prepared to leave, it felt as if we had spent much more time there. Sherlock and I left the library and climbed down the steps of a large, pink marble staircase, waiting for our friend. Lupin lingered at the door to the library.

I could not help but hear the few words that mother and son exchanged above our heads.

"Be careful," Madame Vaudron-Chantal said anxiously.

"Of course, Mama. Of course."

"And . . . Arsène?"

"What?"

"When you see him, greet Theophraste for me."

I was not so indiscreet as to look up over the banister. So I do not know what happened then. But I like to think that before they parted, Arsène and his mother finally hugged each other.

Chapter 15

THE CARDINAL'S CAVERN

Sherlock, Lupin, and I quietly descended from the gentle heights of the *Auteuil*, where Lupin's mother's mansion was located. In the distance, we heard the explosions and booms from the opposite part of the city, in the more populated quarters.

Our inn was on the *rue de Grenelle*, not far from *les Invalides*. It was an area that bore the terrible signs of the Prussian bombing of the previous months. But during those days, it was much calmer than the eastern districts in the city — scenes of the popular uprisings that would soon lead to the birth of the Paris Commune.

As we walked in search of a bite to eat, I found myself thinking of the Grand Master and his plan to silence the din of history, to awaken a dark, ancestral, magical force kept in the heart of St. Michael, no less, and concealed somewhere underneath Paris.

What was going to happen to that city that felt so much my own and I loved with all my heart? I did not really know what to make of the whole story. But I felt a faint shiver run down my spine.

All we could find were some crackers as dry as shards from a clay pot and a chunk of Brie cheese. We decided to go back to our room at the Alchemists to eat, and after a quick venture by Sherlock into a bookseller's shop, we found ourselves back on our pallets, eating our meager snack by candlelight.

Sherlock slipped his hand into his pocket and pulled out what he had bought at the bookseller, a worn-out pocket map of Paris. He spread it out on the floor right away.

"Oh boy, what luxurious service," Lupin joked. "Even a tablecloth!"

The three of us laughed together. After all the excitement of the morning and the somber mood in the streets of the city, we really needed to do so.

Sherlock took the two fragments we had of the ancient map and, a cracker between his teeth, lay down on his stomach, as if he were getting ready to put together a puzzle.

I leaned forward from my pallet to examine the map as well. Lupin had no choice but to do likewise.

"That's the Seine without a doubt, and that line stands for *l'Île Saint-Louis*," Sherlock said, slipping his thin index finger onto a fragment of the ancient map. He put it onto the matching area of the modern map. Despite the roughness of the lines drawn on the old parchment, they clearly matched.

My eyes moved to the second map fragment. On it I saw a tiny inscription:

S. SULP. J.

"This has to be an abbreviation for *Saint-Sulpice*," I said, pointing with my finger.

"Of course, the church over near the Luxembourg," Lupin nodded, placing the parchment fragment on the corresponding spot of the map of Paris.

Sherlock nodded distractedly, examining the map with a doubtful air. After a while, our friend went back to his pallet and stretched out with a deeply disappointed sigh.

"Well? Did we figure something out?" I asked.

"Sure, sure," Sherlock allowed, his eyes on the ceiling. "It's just that I'd hoped to find a connection between those two wretched map pieces and the only other clue we have," he explained.

Lupin and I looked at one another, our eyes bugging out.

"What other clue, please?" I asked.

"The writing on the slip of paper that flew out of Dumas's bundle," Sherlock answered, as if it were the most obvious thing in the world.

"Oh!" Lupin blurted out. "And how much longer were you thinking of waiting before you pulled out the ace up your sleeve?"

Sherlock shrugged. "I thought you'd taken a peek, too. It just read, 'The Cardinal's Cavern.' And in any case, it didn't turn out to be an ace up my sleeve! There's nothing like it on the map, so we're back to square one," he drily concluded.

I hated when Sherlock took on that cold, off-putting manner, but I forced myself not to give it too much weight. Right then, I just wanted to understand more clearly the muddled affair that my friends and I were involved in.

"We're absolutely not back to square one, my friend," I retorted.

Sherlock gave me a searching look.

"We have three new words, if you remember: 'The Cardinal's Cavern,'" I said. "And the fact that they're not marked on the map doesn't mean they can't be an interesting clue."

"Right," Lupin said. "There are loads of Parisians out there. Perhaps 'The Cardinal's Cavern' will mean something to some of them." He indicated outside the window with a nod of his head.

So it was with that, within the space of a few moments, I regained the Sherlock who was dear to me — the one who threw himself into an adventure as soon as he glimpsed a glimmer of action.

★ ★ ★

Sure enough, a few minutes later, the three of us were on the street at the *Place des Invalides*, looking for passersby who we could ask about this mysterious Cardinal's Cavern.

We soon realized we had underestimated the difficulty of the task. A veil of grayish clouds depressed the city, beyond which a pale sun peeped out every so often, like an old silver coin. There was an atmosphere of nervous waiting. Few people were in the streets, and the rare passersby kept right on going without lifting their eyes from the ground. None of them showed the least desire to stop and chat.

Nevertheless, we approached an old priest, a woman with a baby, a large man pulling a cart filled with coal, and a pair of white-haired men — all with the same disappointing results. None of them had heard anything about the Cardinal's Cavern.

That was when I remembered something I had noticed a few hours before when we had been walking back to the Alchemists.

"Follow me!" I said to my friends without thinking about it another second.

I quickly dashed off toward *rue Saint-Dominique*. Just as I remembered, after about a ten-minute walk, Sherlock, Lupin, and I found ourselves standing in front of a rundown building with a worn-out marble sign beside the main entrance. The sign read:

LIBRARY OF ARCHEOLOGICAL STUDIES

What struck me was that in that silent street, where the war seemed to have eliminated all signs of life, a small light was visible inside the dusty library windows. Lupin did not say a word, understanding my plan right away. Together we crossed the shadowy threshold of the building. Despite an oil lamp shining on top of a huge ebony desk, the library seemed deserted.

Lupin coughed a couple of times.

Shortly thereafter, we heard a sound coming from a door behind the desk, and a man soon appeared. His appearance was quite unusual. He should have been very tall, but he was so hunched over that he was barely normal height. His shiny head was bald, and a bushy white mustache drooped across his lips, completely hiding them.

Clearly surprised by the arrival of three people — all together even! — he hastened to slip a monocle onto his right eye.

"Gentlemen . . . Ahem . . . How may I . . ." he said after giving us a long look.

My friends and I looked at each other. Sherlock gave a nod and began to speak. "Please forgive us, sir," he began, with his light French drawl in a typical English accent. "We have something we're curious about — it's perhaps a bit odd — and we would be very grateful if you would help us."

The man seemed impressed by my friend's manners. "Oh, but of course! I would be happy —" he began, when a noise from the hall next door interrupted him.

BOOM!

We all turned together and saw a man trying to remove some of the rubble, taking it from the floor and putting it into his wheelbarrow.

"The war, regrettably," the old librarian said with an air of worry. "You mentioned something you were curious about?"

"Quite right," I confirmed. "My friends and I were wondering if, considering your superior knowledge of the city's antiquities, you might have ever heard mention of a place called the Cardinal's Cavern?"

"The Cardinal's Cavern, eh?" the man repeated, putting his hand to his chin thoughtfully.

Sherlock, Lupin, and I stared at him as if he were an oracle about to speak. But all that came from under his bushy mustache was a deep, thoughtful sigh.

A moment later, the librarian turned toward the little door behind him. "Ferchet?" he called out. "Ferchet?!"

To our surprise, another old man came out, a tiny man with short, tow-colored hair. He could easily have been a contemporary of Voltaire.

"My dear Ferchet," the librarian with the mustache said, turning to his colleague. "These bold young people are looking for information about a place called the Cardinal's Cavern. Does the name mean anything to you?"

The little man looked at us carefully. After thinking intensely for several moments, he replied, "I don't believe I've ever heard that name. But it seems to me that I read it on an old piece of paper that Cardinal Brisy di Lastignac once had at his property near the Bois de Boulogne . . . a page about caves where coal was mined. Therefore, I would interpret the word *caverns* as meaning *mine*. So that would be —"

A flicker of hope had just appeared on Sherlock Holmes's face when the other librarian suddenly interrupted his colleague. "But no, my dear Ferchet! I believe you are remembering incorrectly! The coal mines you are referring to are located on the property of the Count of Grainvilliers, who never wore cardinal's crimson. If anything, you should consider the idea that it has to do with a *cavea cardinalis*, which, if I'm not mistaken . . ."

It took us a few moments to realize that these two good-natured old men were now bogged down in an intellectual discussion, and there was no clear possibility of extracting them from it.

After listening to a couple of long asides on remains from Roman Lutetia, ancient Paris, and the period of Norman domination, Lupin quickly took advantage of a pause. "Thank you, gentlemen. We are extremely grateful. We will treasure all your valuable information!" he said with a deep bow.

The two men seemed a bit disappointed that they would not be able to continue their discussion in front of a small audience, but they nonetheless said goodbye to us cordially. We did the same, trying to hide our disappointment that we had drawn a blank.

We were leaving the library with gloomy faces when we heard a raspy voice behind us.

"Hey! Hey, you!"

As I turned, I have to admit I felt somewhat afraid. A disheveled man with a large ruddy nose was striding after us. When he got closer, I recognized him as the worker we had seen earlier trying to clear away the rubble in the library.

"Hey! I heard you were looking for the Cardinal's Cavern! Is that so?" he asked.

"Yes, good man. You heard right," Sherlock replied, intrigued.

"Oh, well!" the man said. "You see, today's your lucky day then."

"Ah, really?"

"Sure! I know the place, and I can take you there!"

Chapter 16

DESCENT INTO DARKNESS

We looked at each other, unsure of what to do. Then Sherlock gave Lupin and me a look that seemed to say, "What do we have to lose, after all?"

We needed nothing else to decide.

"Well, Mr. . . . ." Lupin started.

"Thomas, but everyone calls me Tomate!" the man said. His smile revealed two rows of crooked, yellowed teeth.

"Well, Mr. Tomate," Lupin then continued. "How much will your . . . gracious company cost us?"

Tomate smiled again. Twisting his felt hat between his hands, he said, "Well . . . I'm glad to do it for you. But of course, if out of generosity . . ."

Lupin pulled a franc coin from his pocket. Twirling it in the air with a flick of his thumb, he caught it on the fly and offered it to Tomate. "Will this generosity do?"

"And how, young man! Tomate now has wings on his feet!" the man rejoiced, grabbing the coin with a predatory grip. And without saying another word, he strode off, signaling us to follow him.

Exchanging a final look, my friends and I went behind him. The man moved through the streets of Paris without hesitation. Very soon we found ourselves along the squalid alleys near the *Place Pigalle*. Little by little, as the streets grew narrower, I felt more and more anxious. Suddenly, after turning a corner, Tomate stopped and pointed to a hovel of sorts. All it had for a door was a filthy curtain.

Two drunkards sat next to the doorway, bellowing an awful song.

I saw Lupin's face flare up with anger in an instant. He went over to Tomate and grabbed him by the collar.

"Perhaps the fact that we're a third of your age made you think we were a bunch of idiots? Eh, Tomate?!"

"Young man . . . I . . . I don't know what you're . . ."

"Arsène, leave him be," Sherlock said. And stretching out his hand to push aside a blanket of ivy tumbling down from the roof, he showed us some writing on the wall, almost erased by time but still legible:

THE CARDINAL'S CAVERN

Lupin let go of Tomate suddenly. Straightening his jacket, Tomate began to grumble.

"Tsk! What manners! Young people . . . It's the last time I give any help to strangers, by the word of old Tomate!"

I apologized to him for my friend's rudeness and gave him a bit more loose change. This seemed enough to lift his spirits again. When Tomate had moved away, the three of us stayed to examine the entrance of that miserable establishment.

"Seeing we've come all the way here, we might as well," Sherlock said. Lupin and I nodded without much enthusiasm.

We entered the Cardinal's Cavern, and all our fears were confirmed. It appeared to be nothing more than a filthy tavern. Its customers were stretched out on the wooden benches or splayed across the tables, and a mammoth innkeeper looked suspiciously at us as soon as he saw us cross the threshold. I could not make heads nor tails of any of it.

"But how could Dumas . . ." was all I could say.

"Maybe they served good sausages here before the war, which our writer found delicious!" Lupin joked, a bitter grin across his face.

Sherlock moved nervously through the big room that comprised the entire premises. He came back to us, shaking his head.

"Sausages or no, there's nothing interesting here," he said, literally leaping toward the entrance.

Lupin and I followed him without saying a word. The day really seemed like one endless, sick prank. As soon as we spotted a trail in our investigation, it turned out to be some sort of vicious joke, leaving us empty-handed.

We turned the corner we had come around and found Sherlock ahead of us, a stunned expression on his face.

"Stop!" he commanded us, hands in the air. "Didn't you see it?"

Lupin and I looked at each other, not understanding.

"Sorry, you saw something? I only heard the sound of hooves and —" Lupin replied.

Sherlock shushed him and cautiously peered around the corner, inviting us to do the same.

"Look!" he hissed.

When I had leaned forward enough to see, I glimpsed

an elegant carriage parked at the entrance to the alley, which was too narrow for it to go in any farther. A tall man had just gotten out. He was wearing a long, dark coat and had a top hat on his head.

"A bit too posh for this dump, don't you think?" Sherlock whispered.

I watched the man with the coat. He seemed to be heading right toward the Cardinal's Cavern. I was about to observe that sometimes aristocrats had secret vices when I saw Lupin's eyes grow wide and his mouth drop.

The man in the alley had stopped in front of the inn's entrance for a moment, briefly showing his face.

"But that . . . that's Montmorency!" Lupin babbled, not believing what he saw.

A beam of light crossed Sherlock's eyes. In the meantime, Montmorency checked his pocket watch and entered the Cardinal's Cavern.

My instinct was to race over and go back into the tavern, but Sherlock held out his arm to stop me.

"Wait!" he said. "All three of us can't go back in. We'll be noticed!"

He quickly slipped off his jacket and tossed it on the ground. Then he untucked his shirt and smeared it with mud from the street. It was not the first time I found myself wondering if Sherlock was completely crazy, but I recall that this time, the thought presented itself especially strongly. What the devil was he doing?

"Wait here!" he ordered us.

Appalled, we watched him run toward the tavern and embrace one of the drunkards seated by the entrance. Singing that dreadful ditty we'd just heard at the top of his lungs, he staggered into the Cardinal's Cavern.

Lupin and I watched, amazed. We had just witnessed another of many sudden transformations skillfully executed by our friend!

Stationed behind the corner, all that was left for us to do was to wait for his return, holding our breath.

We only had to wait a couple of minutes. Then Sherlock, still playing his part, sprang out through the curtain, bellowing something in the direction of the innkeeper. After a couple more yells, our friend made sure there was no one on his heels and rejoined us.

"You won't believe it!" he said. His eyes were bright and sparkling, the way they were when something really intrigued him.

"Well, start telling us about it," Lupin replied.

"When I went into the tavern, I saw Montmorency disappear into the kitchen," Sherlock began.

"And then?"

"Here's the interesting thing — no one was there. And no one came out of there!"

The three of us looked at each other.

"Whatever is back there that's interesting enough to attract the Duke of Montmorency, I'd say is worth our seeing, too!" Lupin said, his eyes laughing.

"You can bet on it!" Sherlock nodded. "But there's a problem. After my latest foray, that elephant of an innkeeper was pretty worked up. I'm afraid he wouldn't appreciate our going back in again."

Lupin replied with a shrug of his shoulders. "If you ladies and gentlemen will allow me to take care of this small obstacle . . ."

Taking the devilish smile that rippled across Lupin's face into account, I knew he was considering something risky and foolish. But in those days, we were guided by recklessness, and so we agreed to his suggestion without hesitation.

In my memory, the image from those next agitated moments was first of Lupin signaling to us to stay outside. Then we heard a shout and the sound of shattering wood coming from the tavern.

"Now!" he then told us, peeking through the curtain.

We raced into the saloon at a run. Inside the Cardinal's Cavern, a huge brawl had exploded, which — I do not even today know how — Lupin had sparked off.

The mammoth innkeeper had flung himself between the opponents to try to calm the crowd, only to wind up involved in the brawl as well. He was not even aware of us sneaking into his kitchen.

We found ourselves in a small, dimly lit room cluttered with cooking pots and dirty plates. Our attention was immediately drawn to a small wooden door next to the fireplace.

Lupin opened it without giving it a second thought.

We saw a flight of stone steps descending into the darkness. Once again we had no doubts. We plunged into that dark throat of stone intending to discover what could be hidden in its gloom. At the bottom of the stairs, Lupin lit a match. Before us stretched a tunnel that smelled of moisture and mold.

"Look!" I exclaimed, noticing something above our heads. Lupin lit a second match. I pointed out the ceiling vault to my friends. There a marble arch ended in a noble coat of arms.

In a few moments, we were back in darkness again. We began walking with great caution, almost on tiptoes.

I felt a hand grab mine. It was Sherlock's. When my eyes grew accustomed to the dark, I noticed a dim glow at the end of the tunnel, toward the left.

Sherlock and Lupin became aware of it, too, and their steps slowed. We tried to act with great care — as much as we could in a situation like that. But it was of little use. I barely realized we had turned a corner when I suddenly found myself dazzled by the light of a torch attached to the wall.

Spotting the silhouette of a hooded man, I could not hold back a scream.

"Halt! Who goes there?" the man commanded.

Lupin went to attack him. But after taking a step, he stopped as still as a statue. The barrel of a revolver had sprung from the wide sleeve of the hooded man's robe.

Chapter 17

THE DARK
HEART OF PARIS

The hooded man stood still, his gun pointed at us. We could not see his face, but we realized he was taking a good look at us.

"What the devil are you doing down here?" he snarled.

Lupin swallowed.

"Here, look . . ." Sherlock murmured, just to stall for time.

I had an idea. I did not know if it was good or bad, but there certainly was not enough time to consider it. So I spoke.

"Oh, sir," I said, whining. "The truth is that we're starving! And we were hoping that the inn's pantry was down here. Don't tell the owner, I beg you! Let us go."

The man stayed silent again and seemed to be considering my words.

After a night at the Alchemists and the rest of our day, our appearances must have fit three starving children.

"All you can find down here is trouble! And if I see you here again, I'll shoot you without thinking twice! Now get lost!" the man warned us, waving the revolver slightly.

We did not need to hear the message repeated. My friends and I darted away, oblivious to the darkness and the uneven floor. When we found ourselves back in the kitchen of the Cardinal's Cavern, we did not even have time to breathe a sigh of relief before the gigantic innkeeper confronted us.

"Ha! Three young crooks! I'm going to teach you now!" he shouted, blocking the way toward the exit and brandishing a large blackened frying pan in front of him threateningly. I saw Lupin spring like a jaguar and grab the innkeeper's arm so that only the bottom of the pan would hit him.

"You've got nothing to teach us, you ball of tallow!" Lupin shouted as the innkeeper fell to the ground, leaving the passage free. Sherlock and I followed our friend's footsteps and left the tavern at a run.

We did not stop running until we were at the banks of the Seine. I pointed out a small grassy bank that sloped gently down toward the river. We reached it and lay down in the grass. Only then, my eyes to the sky, did I realize that the sun had pushed through the clouds. Bright sunlight shone through the trees on the buildings along the river.

Sherlock burst out laughing. "Ball of tallow?" he said. "I wonder where you came up with that!"

Lupin laughed, too. "Well, it's exactly what he looked like, right?"

Even while struggling with that enormous innkeeper, Lupin had been very funny.

"Ball of tallow," I repeated. "Don't you think it would be an excellent title for a short story?"

My friends smiled and agreed with me. But other thoughts, very different ones, were already making their way into our minds.

"That hooded guy," Lupin said thoughtfully. "What the devil was he doing down there?"

"Acting as a guard. That seems obvious to me. And it's clear that someone wants to make sure no one goes in who isn't allowed, as the Duke of Montmorency is, for example," Sherlock said, a blade of grass between his lips.

"But of course . . . the Grand Master!" I said, suddenly popping up onto my knees.

"Oh, boy!" Lupin exclaimed, snapping his fingers. "Perhaps that Grand Master and our hooded friend have already found the path that leads to the Heart of St. Michael's and —"

"And now are ready to start their ritual!" I concluded.

"I doubt it," Sherlock said.

"And might I know why?" I pressed him.

Holmes pulled out the two fragments of the ancient map again and showed us a mark — a very tiny cross sketched in red, which I had first missed.

"It's the only mark this shape and color on the map pieces we have. According to my calculations, it should be right under the Cathedral of Notre-Dame. And there — do you see? At that spot, the underground passages become narrow and tangled. I'm ready to bet that the relic of St. Michael is there!" he said, looking first Lupin and then me in the eyes.

I flinched.

According to my friend Sherlock, we were in possession of the crucial fragment of that ancient map of the Paris underground. The mere idea of it made my heart beat faster.

"But then what was Montmorency doing down there?" I asked at that point.

"Perhaps he was exploring the maze of tunnels, hoping to get lucky even without the complete map," Lupin hypothesized.

"It's possible," Sherlock agreed. "Or else the Grand Master's followers are having a secret meeting down there, to exchange news about how their plan is progressing."

Lupin shook his head, puzzled. "Their plan!" he burst out. "I would really like to understand what it's all about, you know?"

I looked at my friend quizzically.

"I mean . . . the business about the Heart of St. Michael's," Lupin said. "Does this guy, this mysterious Grand Master, really think he can fix a war that has been lost and calm the people of Paris with a relic and who knows what ancient ritual? Bah! Doesn't all this reek a little too much of the Middle Ages to you?" he asked, stretching out on his back across the grass.

"For anyone with a scientific, rational inclination, this whole story sounds quite bizarre, in fact," Sherlock replied.

"But no one who declares himself to be scientific and rational can be so foolish as to deny the existence of forces and powers beyond our understanding," I interrupted, giving Sherlock a pointed look.

"As far as I am concerned, I just want to find out the truth, no matter how unbelievable and surprising it turns out to be," Sherlock responded, paying me back with a cutting glance but then softening it with a slight smile.

"Well said," Lupin approved. "The truth! But then what is the truth of what we saw? For example, how can the passage leading to those hallowed vaults be located in the storerooms of a filthy tavern?"

"The answer, my friend, is in the walls," Sherlock replied mysteriously.

"The walls?!"

"Of course. The walls of the Cardinal's Cavern are ancient, thick, and equipped with sturdy supports. I'm certain that in times past, that place was very different. It was a noble mansion, very probably owned by a family with a cardinal among its members."

"Right," I nodded. That would explain the tavern's curious name. "And then there was that arch at the bottom of the stairs with the coat of arms."

"Of course!" Lupin then exclaimed, sitting up. "Perhaps

it belonged to one of the eight families who divided up the map. Think about it! It's quite reasonable that each of them had access to those underground tunnels, right?"

"Right!" I said, convinced by Lupin's words. "That archway should be a sort of entrance door to —"

"DOOR?!" Sherlock repeated, staring at me wide-eyed. "Good heavens, of course! Door! *JANUA!*" he exclaimed, springing to his feet as if a tarantula had bitten him.

Lupin and I once again found ourselves staring at each other, stunned.

"Could I please know what's going on with you?" Lupin asked him.

"Yes, you're talking strangely . . ." I said.

But Sherlock didn't even seem to hear our words. He stared at the fragment of the map for a few moments, and when he finally looked up, we saw a triumphant look in his eyes.

"On your feet!" he ordered. "Break's over. There's somewhere we have to go now!"

Chapter 18

THE MASTER'S VOICE

"If you say the word *janua* one more time, I swear I'm going to give you a kick in the shin!" I threatened, turning to Sherlock as we walked toward the *rue de Martyrs* at the frantic pace he was setting.

"And I'll follow Irene's example!" Lupin joked.

As we wished, there followed several minutes during which that odd word did not come from our friend's mouth.

"It means *door* in Latin," Sherlock finally explained to us. "And it starts with a *J*!" he concluded, as if that was an extremely exciting piece of information.

"Oh, thank you so much!" I said. "So what?"

"The same letter that's on our map after the abbreviation that stands for *Saint-Sulpice!*" Sherlock said.

Finally, Sherlock's excitement infected Lupin and me as well.

"And so . . . perhaps there's another door at *Saint-Sulpice* — another access to the tunnels!" I said.

"Exactly. And if we're lucky, we won't find a killjoy there like at the Cardinal's Cavern," Lupin added.

Right at that moment, a cart filled with hay came out from a side street heading south, where we also wanted to go. Lupin started to run, gesturing for us to follow him. A few minutes later, we reached the cart and, taking a small leap, arranged ourselves on the back of it, our legs dangling off.

We traveled like that all the way to *Les Halles*, the biggest market in Paris. When we noticed the cart was slowing down, we jumped off. We continued to *Pont Neuf* on foot, which we crossed, finally winding up between the houses along the Left Bank of the Siene.

It did not take us long to arrive near the church of *Saint-Sulpice*, which we promptly headed to, like three cats hunting their prey. A rapid walk around the building showed us that the big portal was locked and barred. But behind the church, something much more interesting was hidden. Just before the altar, built from ancient, worn-out stone and protected by an iron railing, was a small staircase that went down below the ground.

"One hundred francs says that's your *janua!*" Lupin said, pointing to a little door made of dark wood at the bottom of the steps.

Sherlock nodded and shook the gate that gave access to the staircase, pushing on it feverishly. It stayed closed. From our side we saw no lock, only a smooth iron plaque. We looked at it, unsure of what to do, until Lupin took a few steps back. He carefully studied the altar and its gray stone roof.

"Wait here," was all he said. Then he took a short running start, leaping to grab a slender stone molding right below the roof. Next, with one impressive movement, he got a leg onto the roof and finally heaved himself the rest of the way up. At that point, he crawled over the sharp railing and landed at the bottom of the staircase with a final jump. A few seconds later, our friend was climbing back toward us, an amused smile on his face. Out of his jacket pocket, he pulled a ring, which held a number of tools in various shapes and sizes.

"I'm pleased to see you've continued to enhance your collection of picklocks," Sherlock said.

"Well, not to brag, but I think I've got a small talent for this kind of thing," Lupin said, fumbling with the lock. And, almost as if to emphasize his words, a metallic tone indicated that the little gate was open.

Taking a quick look around to make sure no one was in sight, we went down the stairs and waited until Lupin showed us another little example of his talent with the little wooden door.

This lock was a bit harder for our friend, but fewer than ten minutes later we were going down some more stairs, immersed in the darkness of the Parisian underground.

Once we got to the bottom of the staircase, we found ourselves in complete darkness. It smelled moldy and was rather cold. Beyond that, I could not get any clues about the area around us. We stayed still for a moment. Then I heard the sound of a match being struck on the stone, and my two friends' faces appeared in the dark in a halo of dim, yellow light.

We were in a narrow tunnel that had been dug out of the rock. Looking up, I noticed that the arch of the marble roof was every inch the same as the one we had seen at the Cardinal's Cavern. Here, too, a noble coat of arms appeared at the top of the vault.

I looked around. Spotting that sign and blowing out

the match Lupin held between his fingers only took a moment. Then we plunged back into darkness.

"Irene!" Lupin hissed, agitated. "What are you doing?"

"Shhh!" I hissed, as softly as I could. I did not dare add a single word. From somewhere in the darkness of the tunnel, not far from us, I thought I had heard the sound of a voice.

I leaned against the damp, cold rock and kept listening, my heart in my throat. In the frightening silence that followed, I heard Lupin's breath next to me, and I could have sworn I could sense the energetic activity of Sherlock's thoughts.

When I was nearly convinced I had fallen prey to my own suggestion, there it was again: I heard a voice echo again, this time more distinctly. My ears had not tricked me!

I decided to take a step forward, then another. I felt Lupin's hand rest on my shoulder and lightly grab it in encouragement. Then I groped my way for several meters along the rock wall. All of a sudden, I realized that the tunnel had made a turn, beyond which I glimpsed a soft glow. I stopped, uncertain whether to continue. I sensed Sherlock advancing in the dark, moving forward to see around the corner. Following him, I caught sight of a half-open door cut out from the wall. Through the crack, I spied a small portion of the room, lit dimly by a few candles. I saw a hand grab a hooded robe hanging from the wall. Now the voices that reached me were sharp and clearly audible.

" . . . We are very close, my friend! And I think something important will happen soon. I can feel it!" someone said.

"I hope it's as you say, my dear. We don't have much time left. That mob out there is about to take control of the city!"

At that point, we heard fabric rustling and footsteps. The voices grew more distant. A moment later, everything returned to perfect silence.

"Come on! Let's go in!" Lupin whispered.

I wanted to say something, but I saw that my friends had already moved toward the crack to examine the room.

"All clear!" Sherlock hissed.

I took a moment to silence all my thoughts and fears. It was I who had involved Sherlock and Lupin in this story, and I would follow them to see it through.

We widened the crack between the two sides of the door the smallest amount needed to be able to slip inside.

When we were finally in the room, a shiver ran down my spine. It was a dreadfully creepy place — a large, circular room with a few benches placed against the walls and a wooden coatrack. About a dozen dark robes with large hoods hung from it. The only light was from two tall candelabras in the middle of the room.

Looking around, we noticed that in addition to the little door we had come through, there were two arches that led to two corridors facing across from each other.

"Here is where the Grand Master's followers meet!" Lupin said.

"Yes. And I bet the Sacred Order of St. Michael —" Sherlock said, before he suddenly broke off and headed toward the corridor to our right.

The sound of footsteps echoed in the distance.

"Oh, my heavens!" I whispered, putting my hand to mouth. "What now?"

Lupin grabbed two robes from the coat rack and ran to me. "Put one of these on," he said. "It will be okay, you'll see."

I looked into Lupin's eyes for a brief moment, and that was enough to restore my courage.

Sherlock also took a tunic and put it on hurriedly. We had barely turned ourselves into three hooded figures when a portly man entered. He had piggy eyes and long, blondish hair. From his elegant clothing, we gathered he was a nobleman.

I felt Sherlock hastily push me toward the second corridor on the opposite side of the room.

Out of the corner of my eye, I saw the man who had just arrived stop and look at us. With my breath caught in my throat, I grabbed the hem of the robe, which was too long for me, and walked toward the arch.

"Fiat Lux! Fratres!" the man practically shouted in greeting.

Sherlock coughed. His voice as deep as he could make it, he exchanged the Latin greeting with the man, *"Fiat Lux! Frater!"*

I remember thinking — as we passed that doorway and entered the thicker shadows of the corridor — that never like then had the knowledge of a dead language seemed a more exciting asset.

It felt as if I had slipped into the pages of one of those disturbing novels I was so fond of back then, full of gloomy, ruined dwellings and dark secrets. We walked through a long corridor, punctuated by the light of candles placed in small niches along the walls. A confused hubbub came from the end of it, and I thought it must be like the sounds that would rise from the circles of purgatory.

We walked together between the rows of lights in the corridor, and for several moments, I had the sensation that I was dreaming. In fact, it seemed to me that beyond the arch at the end of the corridor lay a dark, stormy sea, which a strange force was dragging me toward.

After a couple more steps, that strange illusion disappeared. What had looked like a stormy sea to me was, in reality, nothing more than an expanse of dark, hooded heads gathered in a large circular room, much like the one we had just left. A hundred followers of the Grand Master, give or take, were gathered in the stone cavern a few steps below us.

"We're finally at their hideout!" Sherlock whispered in my ear. "Now we just have to blend in."

And so we did, climbing down the stairs and trying to stay together in that mass of people.

A few minutes passed. Along the corridor we had come through came other hooded figures, and the hubbub in the semidark chamber kept growing.

Then suddenly, a great commotion erupted from the crowd of hoods. Many voices overlapped, one on top of the other.

"He's coming!"

"Here he is!"

"I see him!"

The light from a torch appeared through a narrow opening in the rock. I rose onto my tiptoes to figure out what was happening, and I saw a man wearing a robe like ours, except in bright red, and wearing an enormous golden necklace. He climbed onto a sort of a pulpit that had been set up in an alcove in the room, accompanied by two other people. On the stone wall behind him hung an old flag of France.

Silence fell in the cavern, and at that moment, we grew certain we were in the presence of the Grand Master. His face stood out from the golden yellow background of the alcove, and he really looked as if he'd come out of a medieval painting.

"*Fiat lux! Fratres!*" he began, with a deep, resonant voice. "Let there be light! And this is not just an empty formula, since very soon, thanks to our courage, the disheartening darkness that France is collapsing into will melt, and an ancient, sacred light will return to illuminate the minds and spirits of the nation! Great, majestic signs are already proclaiming that our victory is near, brothers! The star of Sirius and the other radiant stars in the constellation Virgo are in a favorable position. Very soon, you can be sure, our quest for the fragments of the ancient map of the Order will come to its conclusion. Then we shall know where the holy relics are safeguarded, and our days of fear shall come to an end! No longer will we have to see Paris — already crushed by Prussian boots — wind up in the hands of criminals. We, the reconstituted Sacred Order of St. Michael, will lead the city and the nation to salvation — certainly not Mr. Adolphe Thiers and all the cowards in Versailles who follow him . . ."

While the man in the red robe launched into an impassioned rant against Thiers and his followers, we could not help but notice that unlike the Grand Master, whose face stayed in darkness, the two figures at his side seemed happy to show their real faces to the crowd. I had no difficulty recognizing the person on his right, the Duke of Montmorency. But I felt profoundly worried when I recognized the figure standing to the left of the Grand Master.

It was a woman. *That* woman! The mysterious lady I had met in the gardens of the Evreux cathedral.

I wanted to share my discovery with my friends, but despite feeling troubled, I realized it would be too foolish and remained silent.

However, I was not the only one to notice how the woman craved attention. I clearly heard a hooded figure next to me saying, "That lady certainly gives herself airs!"

I thought it a good opportunity to gather information, and so, speaking through the heavy fabric of my robe, I said, "That woman doesn't know what modesty is!"

"Don't expect anything else from Madame de Valminier," the person next to me whispered scornfully. "She tricked poor old Duke d'Aurevilly, and with the tiny bit of power she got from that, she's now vying with Montmorency to get into the Grand Master's inner circle! He'll soon become France's new leader, and she —"

"SHHH!" hissed someone behind us. My neighbor grew silent.

Meanwhile the Grand Master's voice continued thundering in my ears. A harrowing question came to mind. What did Madame de Valminier's reference to my family during our meeting mean?

A sudden thought struck me like a blow to the heart. I looked around, shaken. Perhaps under one of those dark hoods would be hiding . . . my father? But if my father was involved in this business of the Order of St. Michael, why had that woman come to see me?

The echoes of these questions were still ringing in

my mind when I heard the Grand Master dismiss his followers. His speech had ended. The hum from before started up again, and the hooded figures began streaming toward the corridors. I, however, stayed still, captivated by thoughts of my family's secrets, however dark and troubling.

Then I felt myself swept away by that river of people. As if suddenly aroused from sleep, I realized that Sherlock and Lupin were no longer next to me. To get back to them, I moved abruptly and tripped on my long robe. I found myself on the ground, hood around my shoulders and face uncovered. Unfortunately for me, I had fallen near one of the big candelabras, which lit my face.

"Who the devil is this little girl?" one of the hooded people yelled, pointing at me. In a few instants, I was surrounded.

Sherlock and Lupin immediately pushed their way through the wall of people to come to my rescue.

"Leave her alone!" Sherlock shouted.

Lupin helped me get back up. With the use of our elbows, we fought our way toward the corridor. We were about to take off at a run when three hooded figures blocked our way, pulling out their pistols.

"I wouldn't take another step if I were you!"

Chapter 19

AN EMPEROR

It was one of the most awful moments in my life. My heart filled with anger and shame for how I had gotten my friends into trouble by tripping and falling on the ground like a fool. I still remember the shouts from the hooded crowd behind us.

"Scoundrels!"

"They're plants sent by the rebels!"

"Yes! Teach them a good lesson!"

The Grand Master's guards ordered us to raise our hands. They escorted us toward a tiny door in the middle of the corridor, guns pointed at our spines. Then they forced us to walk through a short, damp corridor. At its end was a filthy cell, which they abruptly shoved us into. I had just gotten back up when one of the guards grabbed me to search me.

"Don't you dare, worm!" Lupin attacked the guard, flinging himself on top of him.

One of the Grand Master's other cronies hit him in the face with the butt of his gun and drove him into the corner.

"No!" I screamed.

"We're not here for a romantic comedy, sonny, so see that you cut out this nonsense!"

Then they searched the three of us. In Sherlock's pockets, the Grand Master's men found the two fragments of the map. Everything is blurry from the moment I saw one of the hooded men grip the two pieces of parchment between his hands, as my eyes filled with tears.

Nonetheless, I heard one of our jailers say to another, "Call the boss! Right away!"

The remaining two guards tied our wrists together with pieces of rope. After they locked the door with a heavy chain and a bolt, they disappeared into the dark corridor.

"I'm . . . I'm so . . . I'm so sorry," was all I could whisper between my sobs.

"You needn't apologize for anything, Irene," Lupin said. He began to rub the rope tying his hands together against a rock that stuck out from the wall.

"Right. It's not over yet," Sherlock added.

Looking back, the most amazing thing is that my friends' faces showed they were not just saying this to comfort me. For Sherlock, this affair was truly like a chess game still being played. For Lupin, it was like a boxing match in which our opponent had scored a good hit but was far from having knocked us to the canvas. If, on the one hand, that relieved me a bit, on the other hand, the thought of having gotten my two extraordinary friends into trouble was like a thorn jabbing into my pride. Even today, many years later, it hurts.

Luckily, I did not have to remain at the mercy of these thoughts for very long. After a few minutes, we saw the Grand Master's red robe appear beyond the bars of our cell. In his hands, he was carrying the two map fragments that his guards had just taken from us, and he had his hood lowered to his shoulders. I could see his face and was amazed. He was only a young man, with reddish hair, thin whiskers, and intense, brilliant blue eyes. A smile that was both vicious and mocking seemed to animate every muscle in his face.

"I don't know who you are, my dear children," he said, waving the pieces of parchment. "But I'm delighted you decided to pay me a visit!"

Then he burst into laughter and walked away, escorted by his men.

I watched them disappear into the darkness until I no longer could see them. Then I turned to my friends. I saw right away that Sherlock had been struck by his appearance, too.

"He's really not what I expected!" I said, almost without thinking.

Sherlock began pacing back and forth in the cell nervously. "You're right." He nodded. "There's something strange about that man!"

"If you mean to say you expected he would be a stern old man with a white beard, well, I admit you're right," Lupin said as he continued to work on the rope tied around his hands.

"His tone of voice, his cadence . . ." Sherlock continued. "When he spoke in front of all of his followers it was different, as if . . ."

" . . . as if he was putting on an act!" I anticipated.

"Exactly. And then . . ."

"And then?"

"In his speech he made a basic astronomy error," Sherlock said.

"Oh. Really?"

"Sure. He said Sirius was part of the constellation Virgo, but it belongs to the Big Dog."

"Goodness," I said. "So not only was he merely performing, but he didn't even learn his script very well!"

Lupin snorted, and with one last effort, he finally managed to loosen the rope enough to free his hands.

"Maybe that man is not a walking encyclopedia — agreed," he said, rubbing his reddened wrists. "But the thing that worries me is that his thugs are armed to the teeth. So I would say it's a case of —"

At that exact moment, Sherlock abruptly stopped in the middle of the cell and put his index finger to his lips, motioning Lupin to be silent.

"Quiet! I hear something!" Sherlock said. Looking around, he pointed to a dark little corner of the cell. "Up there! Quick!" Sherlock stretched his hands toward Lupin, who helped him get the rope off, and then said, "Help me get up to that corner."

Lupin asked no questions. Ducking down, he grabbed Sherlock by the knees and lifted him up to the place he had been pointing to.

Holmes put his ear next to a little hole in the rock, closing his eyes so that he could concentrate on listening.

I stared at his thin, pointy face. It was tense from the effort of grasping as much of what he was hearing through that crack as he could. With every little tremor and every little contraction in his face, my heart beat faster. He spent some time up there, which seemed very long, but in reality it was only a few minutes. Then suddenly Sherlock gestured to Lupin to put him down.

"They're coming back!" he whispered.

Both of them hid their hands behind their backs and leaned against the wall, pretending to be tied up still.

We heard the sound of steps, and shortly thereafter, the Grand Master and his friends reappeared beyond the bars.

"So what should we do with them?" said one of the thugs.

The Master threw us another cursory look.

"Our young friends? Leave them there inside a while to cool their heels," he said. "We have more important things to deal with."

And without saying anything else, he disappeared again, with the nervous pace of someone who has important matters waiting for him.

As soon as the echo of his footsteps vanished from the corridor, Lupin and I went over to Sherlock.

"What did you hear?" I asked him, while Lupin undid the rope around my wrists.

Sherlock looked very thoughtful and waited a little before responding.

"They had just put the map back together. The Grand Master was thrilled, to say the least," he said. "And yet I'm sure he ordered the guards to say nothing about it to his followers. They were not to know anything."

"What do you mean by that?" Lupin jumped on him. "Isn't that exactly what those masked lordlings were waiting for?"

"It is," Sherlock confirmed. "But our Master doesn't want this discovery shared with his followers and . . ."

At this point, Sherlock broke off and shook his head, perplexed.

"I think I know French pretty well, and yet I didn't understand the word he used to refer to them."

"Maybe you didn't hear correctly," I suggested.

"On the contrary. He said the sentence in a loud voice, and I heard it perfectly well. He said, 'Those *bardouchis* shouldn't know anything about it!'"

Lupin stifled a guffaw.

Sherlock and I turned to look at him, surprised. Not even I, who had grown up in France, had ever heard that word.

"You must have heard wrong, my friend," Arsène said.

"Out of the question," Sherlock said. "I have very acute hearing, and I don't have the slightest doubt about what I heard. Why do you think I'm wrong, though?"

"Simple. Because that word *bardouchi* is used by Belgians — and not even by all of them. Only in a certain part of Belgium would you happen to hear someone who uses that term to talk about someone who has a screw loose."

"And how do you know something like that?" Sherlock asked.

"Simple. It so happens that that I'm unlucky enough to have my Uncle Constant, who lives in that small corner of Belgium, which would be a small southern city named Namur —"

Upon hearing the name of that city, Sherlock's forehead wrinkled. He muttered, "Namur . . . Namur . . . Namur . . ." He then stayed quiet for several moments until he took again to repeating, "Namur . . . Namur . . ."

"So do you mean to torture us as you recently did with that Latin?" I teased him, intrigued.

But he did not even reply and continued his recitation, "Namur . . . Namur . . ."

All of a sudden his muscles tensed up. A flash of light went across his eyes, which stayed still, like dark glass beads. Once again Sherlock repeated as if possessed, "NAMUR!"

"Right," Lupin joked. "And I don't get how hearing the name of the most boring city in this world could have this effect on you!"

Sherlock smiled a fleeting smile, as if he had been bewitched. "It's funny . . . It's the only thing I know about this Belgian city. And yet, this one tiny thing just allowed me to figure out . . . everything. Everything, do you understand?"

"No, I don't have even any idea of what you're raving about!" I burst out.

Sherlock looked at me, with that strange, triumphant smile still on his face. "Look . . . the only thing I know about Namur — and it took me a while to bring it into focus — is that it's the city that gave birth to Albert Vaneighem. Or, if you prefer the nickname that the newspapers coined for him . . . the Emperor of Con!"

Chapter 20

THE DARKEST TRUTH

"A . . . a con man?" I stammered, suspecting I had heard Sherlock's last words incorrectly.

"The best of all of them," he confirmed. "One who managed to sell an American tycoon an island that didn't exist and equipment for telepathic communication to the Swedish king. It actually was just a metal chest, to be perfectly clear."

Lupin was even more astonished than I was. "So you think this Vaneighem could be the Grand Master?!" he said, dumbfounded. "And you figured all that out just from *bardouchi*? A word my Uncle Constant uses to make fun of my father?"

Sherlock shrugged. "We never know whose hand will open the door to the truth," he said, citing some poet. "Plus, think about it! This way everything makes sense. His appearance, which is so out of place, the voice that changes when he addresses his followers, the basic error in astronomy . . . It explains everything if he's not what he says he is, but rather just a swindler who's juggling a huge act."

On the one hand, Holmes's theory seemed like total nonsense. On the other hand, the more I thought about that man, the more likely the story seemed. The face I had seen a little earlier was that of a shrewd con man and certainly not that of a dark sorcerer!

Many things, however, were still shrouded in mystery.

"But even if the Grand Master is Vaneighem, what would a man like him want with a saint's relic?" I asked.

"We can't know that yet," Sherlock admitted. "But I'm willing to bet he has his reasons for getting hold of it."

Lupin snickered sharply. "Underneath, it's not so hard to believe you. This business of hooded people underground always seemed like a big masquerade to me! And now, what do you say about going out there to find out if you're right?" he asked, going up to the padlock on our cell.

While Lupin got working with his tools, Sherlock and I crouched down on the ground, our eyes set on our friend. The big padlock holding us prisoner, however, was not scrap metal like the lock at *Saint-Sulpice*. It resisted all of Lupin's attempts.

★ ★ ★

Time passed, marked by poor Arsène's curses. In the corridor beyond the bars, the torch that had been providing us with a little light was slowly dying out.

During those rough-and-tumble days in Paris, we had eaten very little. I felt faint, and my throat felt parched from thirst. As the darkness around us grew thicker, I slipped into sleep more than once, falling prey every time to short but scary nightmares.

Finally, Lupin's voice came from my right. "I've got it! I did it!" he whispered in the darkness.

I found it hard to believe, but it was true. The padlock had finally yielded, and we were free to leave that horrible cell. We slipped past the bars and lined up single file, Lupin at the front and Sherlock at my back. It seemed as if this part of the underground had been abandoned, and we'd been forgotten in the cell. Being considered simple, defenseless children had for once been a benefit to us.

And so it would have been crazy not to take advantage of the opportunity to escape.

We moved silently, as carefully as we could, holding our breath at every corner we turned. Lupin retraced the steps we had taken in the afternoon when we came from the church of *Saint-Sulpice*, but when we found ourselves in the large circular chamber, we got an unpleasant surprise. The little door we had passed through on the way in was now locked with two sturdy bolts.

"No!" Lupin swore between his teeth.

We had no choice. Nothing else remained for us other than to go on through the dark tunnels that were unfamiliar to us.

Sherlock snatched a small surviving stub of candle from a candelabra and fixed it to his little pocket notebook so we would have a little bit of light for our walk. We wandered for long minutes through those dank stone passages, one so much like the next that more than once I thought we were passing through a section where we had already been.

We found ourselves at the opening to a corridor that was larger than the others when we heard the sound of steps thundering, leading us to believe they belonged to a group of well-fed people.

"This way! Quick!" Sherlock said. He blew out the candle.

We stopped after a few steps and hid ourselves in a dark nook that had moisture seeping into it.

The steps grew closer. From the little alcove, I saw dark shapes silhouetted in the orange halo of several torches.

The group stopped abruptly.

"Are you sure this is the right way?" someone asked.

"I swear it to you, sir," replied a woman's voice that made me shudder for some reason. I covered my mouth with my hand, wondering what in that voice had disturbed me so much.

And it was right then that I asked myself yet again during this adventure if I was dreaming, despite the fact that I had my eyes wide open. For in the flickering light of the torches, I actually thought I saw Mr. Nelson's features. When the small company turned to move forward, my impression became a certainty.

"Mr. Nelson!"

My voice gushed from my mouth without my being able to control it. Instinctively, I took a few steps forward.

"Good gracious! Miss Irene!" our butler exclaimed, running to meet me. I found myself in his arms, stunned.

"Mr. Nelson . . . It's such a delight to see you again!" I said.

"Oh, Irene . . . Thank heavens," murmured a woman's voice, one different from the voice I had heard a few moments before. And after those words, the woman who had spoken them burst into tears. I was extremely surprised and quickly turned to face her. She was a slender woman with delicate features . . . *Had I seen her before, perhaps? Or was it a trick of the dim light?* But there was no time to think about it.

Sherlock and Lupin were now a step behind me. I saw Mr. Nelson rest his icy gaze on them.

"You!" he exclaimed harshly. "You . . ."

"Mr. Nelson, I beg you," I interrupted. "It's not what you think. Everything that happened was my fault alone!"

There were many more things I would have liked to say and should have said to Mr. Nelson, but there was no way I could then.

A tall, slightly bent-over man came a few steps nearer, affectionately patting the hand of the woman in tears. "My name is Jean-Jacques d'Aurevilly, and to have found you and your friends, is for me a cause for great relief and joy. There will be time to talk about it later. First, however, I believe we should leave this place now."

The voice of that no-longer-young man seemed filled with wisdom, and no one had any objection.

As we walked through the dark tunnels lit by the two torches, I lingered to study the little group we'd been united with. Besides Mr. Nelson, d'Aurevilly, and the lady who had burst into tears, I counted at least four armed men walking ahead of us.

Turning briefly, I saw that there were another two armed guards behind me. Between them was another woman wearing a bonnet and a large scarf that hid her face. I was deeply curious to find out who she was, but my desire to breathe a little fresh air — outside the underground — was even greater. For this reason, I kept walking quickly next to Mr. Nelson and my friends, trying not to think of all the questions I wanted to get answered right then.

One step after the other, I felt that horrible adventure under the earth ending. As my relief grew bit by bit, I started to think about the explanations I would have to give, first and foremost, to my father and my mother.

So I was silent and deep in thought when I heard a voice echoing from a side passage.

"Confound it! We need at least two sticks of dynamite and . . ."

All I know is that a few moments later I found myself in Sherlock's arms, while all around me it seemed as if bedlam had erupted.

Our little company suddenly found itself faced by the Grand Master and two of his henchmen. The wretches immediately grabbed their weapons. The Duke d'Aurevilly's guards did the same, meeting them with rifles.

"Don't be foolish!" the head of the guards shouted. "We're seven armed men against two! Put your revolvers on the ground."

After an irritable nod of their leader's head, the Master's men did as they were ordered.

"May I at least know who is viciously attacking me?" the man in the red robe roared.

"My name is Jean-Jacques François d'Aurevilly and I, too, would very much like to know to whom I am speaking," the ancient nobleman said, taking a step forward.

"Here is the answer for your satisfaction: I am Ermete Crusius, Grand Master of the Sacred Order of St. Michael and Knight —"

"Why not cut it short and state that you're really Mr. Albert Vaneighem?" Sherlock interrupted.

The Master's eyes darted to my friend's face, showing a brief flash of surprise. But the man seemed skilled at hiding any mood. And his mouth immediately stretched into a scornful smile.

"You again . . . But you're not entirely wrong underneath. There's no reason to continue this farce," he said. He turned toward the duke. "And if you're really the Duke d'Aurevilly that I've heard so much about, I know you're certainly a shrewd, reasonable man. Someone I won't need to play the role of a mysterious sorcerer for. So, yes, I am Albert Vaneighem, and I'm sure I can make you a very advantageous offer."

"What offer are you blabbering about?" d'Aurevilly retorted furiously.

"If we join forces, we may soon be able to put our hands on an extremely valuable object, one able to guarantee us both immense richness. Isn't that a generous offer?"

Right then, the woman in the bonnet stepped forward, emerging from the darkness where she had stayed hidden until then. She tore the scarf away from her face, and I finally realized she was Madame de Valminier.

"How . . . What . . . What are you saying, Master? I . . . I don't understand . . ." she stammered, her face white as a sheet.

Vaneighem gave her a crueler look than I had ever seen, full of hate.

"YOU!" he screamed. "I should have guessed your stupidity would ruin everything!" An unrepeatable word followed.

The woman's tear-filled eyes seemed to freeze, so great was her dismay.

However, d'Aurevilly looked at the woman with great pity. Whispering a few words in her ear, he invited her to move away again.

Then he turned back to Vaneighem, his eyes shining with disdain.

"My dear sir, you know nothing about me, while I have the debatable fortune to know about your evil deeds from the newspapers! Ever since the first time I heard about this mysterious Grand Master, I suspected it was some sort of fraud, but now that I know what a miserable scoundrel is involved, it will be an even greater pleasure for me to help you get the end you deserve!"

Vaneighem did not appear to react and merely gave the duke a scornful smile.

"Well, then I guess that —" he started to say in an incredibly calm voice.

At exactly that instant, springing like a lightning bolt, the con man jumped backward into the dark passage we had seen him come from. Holding the edge of an old barrel that had been hidden in a dark corner, he hurled it at d'Aurevilly's guards. Terrible confusion ensued. The duke's men, caught by surprise, fired random shots. I remember the cries, the clouds of dust, and the splinters of stone whistling through the air. And then Lupin, moving quickly, jumped over the little barrel and a guard on the ground, giving chase to the con man.

"Arsène!" I screamed. I wanted to lunge down the passage, too, but Sherlock stopped me, grabbing me by the arm.

It's hard for me to find the words to describe how I felt when I saw the Master's red robe reappear. Vaneighem's face was twisted into a horrible sneer. Lupin was at his back, holding his arm in a grip that must have been quite painful and that kept the man at his mercy.

"Thank you, young man!"

"Well done!"

Mr. Nelson and the head of the guards congratulated him, taking charge of the imposter.

His henchmen, however, were able to make a run for it, taking advantage of the confusion. No one cared too much about that insignificant detail.

D'Aurevilly's guards tied up Vaneighem's hands and surrounded him.

SHERLOCK, LUPIN & ME

"You're just a pretentious old man, and your days are numbered! The rebels will make mincemeat out of you!" the Emperor of Con yelled. But no one listened any longer, not even the recipient of these insults, the Duke d'Aurevilly. Instead, the Duke gently grasped the sobbing Madame de Valminier.

Despite having run into serious danger due to this woman, I could only feel great pity for her.

As the guards escorted Vaneighem, Sherlock and Lupin enjoyed his insults as if they were the most delightful entertainment. I walked along beside them and could not help smiling, despite all the thoughts spinning through my mind.

Finally we reached a small stone staircase, which brought us into the open air. We emerged into a garden, next to a brick building that looked like a stable to me. The afternoon clouds had cleared, and a nearly full moon shone in the sky. The guards took custody of Vaneighem, leading him to a small annex with sturdy iron grating on the windows.

For a little while, Mr. Nelson stayed beside the woman who had burst into tears upon seeing me, down in the underground. The woman kept looking at me, even then, with eyes that seemed to shine with great emotion.

I looked at her carefully as well, and in a flash, I realized I knew her.

Of course! She was the mysterious lady who had chanced to meet me several times in her carriage in Saint-Malo during the previous months, at the opera house and along the streets of London. I thought about how much her face beneath the moonlight resembled the delicate feminine profile on the cameo she had given me this past Christmas.

I took two steps toward her, intending to speak to her and finally discover who she was. But for a reason I cannot explain, I suddenly stopped in the middle of the street. Right then, we met each other's eyes. Like me, she too had fallen prey to hesitation. So we looked at each other, smiling, without even saying a word.

Chapter 21

AN EXTRAORDINARY DAY

We discovered that the garden was part of the mansion belonging to the Duke d'Aurevilly, who gave instructions for bedrooms to be made ready for every one of us. We were all very tired and grateful to the duke for his hospitality.

When it came time to say goodnight, the lady from the cameo came over to me in the mansion's large front hall. She offered me a silk nightgown in a bright azure color.

"Perhaps it's a little big for you, but I think it's better than nothing," she said, smiling at me. Bidding me good night, she moved away and went down the grand marble staircase that led to the bedrooms.

When I was finally alone in the room I had been given, however, I tried to collect my thoughts, which were now more tangled than ever. My great exhaustion kept me from doing so, however, and I fell into a deep, dreamless slumber almost immediately.

The next day, I arose in the late morning, well rested and feeling a bit calmer.

What had happened that was so serious, after all? I asked myself now, comforted by the light of a new day. Of course, I had disobeyed my parents and made them worry. I was now old enough to know that every action had its consequences, and I knew it would be true for me in this case. There were rules to the game, and I was prepared to accept them. Yet on the other hand, had I not always been right to say that my life had been shrouded in mystery? My parents could not deny that, and I hoped that this would make my behavior a little more understandable in their eyes.

I found an old silver hairbrush on a table and used it to deal with my hair, which had great need of it after the last few days. Then I got dressed and went downstairs, intending to go look for Mr. Nelson.

There was no trace of him to be found. But I heard voices coming from a room to the right of the marble staircase. The door was ajar. I knocked and heard the voice of the Duke d'Aurevilly inviting me to enter.

I found myself in a large dining room. The duke was seated at the table with Sherlock and Lupin. The duke politely asked me to join them for lunch. Feeling attacked by hunger pangs, I accepted with pleasure.

After a maid poured me a cup of *café au lait* and I served myself a slice of buttered bread and apricot preserves, the duke gave me a kindly look.

"Your friends have been telling me about your adventures of the past few days!" he said. "You three young people are remarkably brave!"

"Perhaps the three of us are just reckless," I suggested.

The duke laughed heartily. "After all, that's natural! You are young, and you threw yourselves headlong into this matter, which was so distant from your lives, at heart. Whereas I, a poor worn-out old man, kept hiding my head in the sand, even though not a day passed without someone coming to speak to me about this Grand Master." He shook his head. "Oh, you should not believe that my old nose hadn't smelled a rat in this story! I certainly had. But at my age, you get like this, closed into your own shell, wanting the world just to leave you in peace."

"Nonetheless, you didn't swallow Vaneighem's bait," Lupin said. "And that's undoubtedly to your credit."

"Perhaps," d'Aurevilly said. "But I have much to blame myself for. Particularly if I think of poor Charlotte . . . Madame de Valminier, I mean."

"Why, if it's not indiscreet of me?" I asked.

"You see, Charlotte is a distant cousin of my poor wife. The daughter of a genuine fiend. He squandered all he had and left her without a penny. So my wife took her under her protection, and Charlotte has lived with us for many years. When my wife passed away, she left her a small income. Charlotte has always been a naïve young woman, wanting to take revenge on the life that treated her so poorly. When she started to talk only about the Grand Master and his noble plan to save Paris and all of France, I should have been worried. Instead I did nothing more than grumble a few insults," d'Aurevilly said, lowering his gaze.

We heard him sigh deeply, but when he raised his head again, his smile had returned.

"Luckily, three young adventurers came to settle this ugly affair! Isn't that so?" he joked.

"We were just in the right place," Sherlock said. "The truth tumbled between our feet like a stone. Although there are still a few things that aren't completely clear to me."

"Indeed? And yet I thought you were the one who first figured out who the devil this Grand Master really was — or am I mistaken?"

"No, you're not mistaken, sir," Sherlock admitted, with all his immodesty. "What I don't understand is the reference Vaneighem made to an extremely valuable object when he was talking to you. As far as I know, there should have been a relic down there. An object that surely is worth something!"

"The Heart of St. Michael. No, my young friend, but the chest that holds it . . . Ah! That certainly is worth something!"

"A chest?" Lupin asked, intrigued.

"Of course! That was one of my grandfather Duke Joseph's favorite stories! He loved to tell me about when King Charles VII was returning from a lucky military campaign and a priest gave him the relic of St. Michael, believed to have been lost before then," d'Aurevilly explained. "And so the sovereign decided to hide it in a secret place in the Paris underground, so that it would protect his beloved capital. He had it set into a chest, and he had the Stars of Africa mounted on it. At that time, the Stars of Africa were the largest rubies known to exist . . . and their value today is nearly incalculable!"

Sherlock, Lupin, and I looked at each other. Now the series of events made some sense. But it still was not all clear to me.

"And the story about the map being divided into eight fragments?" I asked.

D'Aurevilly smiled. "Charles VII was a clever man, believe me! When it came time to put the relic underground, he decided to keep the place he had chosen a secret. A secret from everyone, except eight representatives of the oldest and most prominent noble families in France. He made them knights of the newly reborn Order of St. Michael, as well as guardians of the Map of the Order. These included the Dukes of Prunes and Alençon, the Viscount of Rochechouart and, obviously, one of my ancestors." At that point, the duke paused and considered us again. "Do you have any idea why he did such a thing, my young friends?" he asked slyly.

"Because by telling those gentlemen about such a solemn secret, he intended to create strong bonds of loyalty and obedience, I presume," Sherlock responded, without the slightest hesitation.

"Exactly, young man!" d'Aurevilly nodded, admiring my friend's promptness. "That way, he strengthened his relationships with those families, and, consequently, his own power."

Unlike what usually was the case, I appreciated that little history lesson. Lupin took on a dubious air, however.

"What you just told us is perfectly reasonable, Sir Duke," he admitted. "But then, how did Vaneighem take in so many people with his sham about the Grand Master?"

"Oh! That is easy, my boy. He had a very powerful ally — a popular, centuries-old legend. When you understand men's souls better, you'll see that all it takes is a large number of people inclined to believe, and a legend suddenly becomes truth. And unfortunately, this time many noble Parisians — their hearts filled with fear — wanted nothing more than to believe in the fable of the Grand Master."

"And now? What do you plan to do with the relic?" Sherlock asked him.

"Absolutely nothing at all!" the duke replied. "Other than leave it resting in its place in the heart of Paris."

"I'm afraid, though, that King Charles's secret is no longer so secret," I broke in. "We also know that the Heart of St. Michael is located under the Cathedral of Notre-Dame. And all of Vaneighem's accomplices know it now, too!"

The duke looked me in the eyes. I realized he was about to tell me something he had never confided to anyone. "I do not think you need to worry too much about that, my dear," he said. "The crypt where the relic is kept cannot be reached from inside the cathedral, and many of the underground passages below there have collapsed over the centuries."f

"Actually, I believe Vaneighem himself met this problem," Sherlock added. "During our final eventful encounter, I'm sure I heard him talk about explosives. That's the only way to open a path through the collapsed passages, I imagine."

"Just so. Not to mention that the Map of the Order is now back in good hands," the duke said, patting the breast pocket of his dark tailcoat.

And his words rang out like the conclusion of that tumultuous Parisian adventure.

My friends and I were leaving the room when the duke turned back to us. "So tell me, with regards to

Notre-Dame, have you ever seen Paris from the top of the North Tower?" he asked. "It's a fantastic sight. Quite different from moldy passages! It's something your young eyes ought to see."

The duke's words pressed me to imagine the city he was offering us — immense before my eyes, extending to the horizon as far as the eye could see.

"It would truly be wonderful to be able to go up there," I said.

"Why not go then?" the duke suggested. "I can make my carriage available to you, and you will be there in ten minutes!"

I knew that the time for explanations would come very soon, and almost certainly alongside punishment for my recent poor conduct. So the idea of having one last moment of freedom filled me with enthusiasm. Sherlock and Lupin must have sensed this, because after hesitating for an instant, they accepted the duke's offer with gratitude.

D'Aurevilly clapped his hands in satisfaction and stood up, inviting us to follow him out to the courtyard. When we were outside the mansion, Mr. Nelson approached us.

"I just received a message from your father. He will be here this afternoon. So it would be appropriate if you were back here in no more than a couple of hours," Mr. Nelson said to me, casting an eye at the carriage waiting for us.

"Of course, Mr. Nelson. I promise. We'll be back in time," I said. And I climbed into the carriage with my friends.

Duke d'Aurevilly gave his coachman instructions and then said goodbye to us, smiling. And when we finally got going, we found ourselves alone again, just the three of us.

"Hey, but . . . doesn't it bother you not to have seen the relic or especially that chest?" Lupin asked. "I mean, with those blasted rubies, it should be an extraordinary object!"

"I suppose so," I replied. "But I'd prefer a bit of fresh air at the top of the tower of Notre-Dame now. I hope I'm done with tunnels and underground passages for a little while!"

Sherlock yawned loudly. "As far as I'm concerned, now that we've gotten to the bottom of this business, those rubies are just like any other minerals. But I'm looking forward to my return trip to London! I think I'm going to have one of the most interesting conversations of my life, do you know?"

"Ah, really?"

"Absolutely. The Duke d'Aurevilly is not sure what will happen in Paris in the coming days. So after having sent a telegram to Scotland Yard, he decided to escort Vaneighem to London, where he's sought after for at least a half dozen crimes," Sherlock crowed.

"You don't mean to tell me that you —"

"You bet! I will take advantage of the passage and will be traveling in the midst of that mixed company," he replied.

"A trip side by side with that gallows bird? I wouldn't do it for all the gold in the world!" I said.

"He's a perfect rogue, we're in agreement there. But for someone interested in crime, Vaneighem is truly a fountain of information."

At that point, Lupin let out a long sigh. "Tomorrow I am going to have a conversation with my father. He's not exactly a saint either, but I'm afraid I won't enjoy it very much."

Sherlock and I burst out laughing. After Arsène's witty remark, we climbed out of the carriage in an excellent mood and headed toward the majestic cathedral.

Unlike *Saint-Sulpice*, Notre-Dame was open, although completely empty. We followed the duke's directions and, at the start of the right nave, found a narrow spiral staircase that wound up the North Tower.

We tackled it almost at a run, eager to emerge at the top. I found myself at the front, and when I finally reached the end of the stairs . . . I jumped and let out a scream. Before me stood a monstrous figure. It looked at me with a diabolical grin.

My friends joined me in a flash.

Right away, I heard Sherlock's unmistakable cackling. "Apparently you're not a fan of Mr. Viollet-le-Duc!" he teased.

Hearing the name was enough for me to understand what had happened. The creature who had greeted me up there was nothing more than a gargoyle, one of the disturbing statues that the architect Viollet-le-Duc had placed at the top of the north tower of the cathedral during his recent restorations.

That funny misunderstanding enlivened our happy visit. The time spent up there with Sherlock and Arsène, watching Paris stretched out before us along the winding course of the Seine, is one of the most beautiful, intense memories that I have kept of our friendship. It stays with me even today.

So it was with great regret that I asked them to climb

back down and return to the d'Aurevilly mansion. As much as I'd wanted to stay, I had no intention whatsoever of breaking my word to Mr. Nelson.

In front of the cathedral, just as the duke had arranged, we found the carriage, which brought us back to the mansion. Sherlock would not be leaving for London with Vaneighem and the guards before nightfall, and we resolved to meet again before he left for a final farewell.

Waiting for me on the stairs to the mansion, I found neither Mr. Nelson nor my father, but rather the lady from the cameo.

"Good day, Irene," the woman greeted me. "Your father sent a telegram saying that he would be a few hours late."

"Ah, I understand. Thank you very much for passing the message to me," I replied with a curtsy, preparing to climb the stairs.

But the woman placed a slender, delicate hand on my arm. "Irene," she said, after a deep sigh. "Do you mind if we take advantage of this time to . . . talk?"

"No, of course not. On the contrary, I would be very happy to do so," I replied, unable to look away from her anxious eyes.

The woman accompanied me to a sitting room on the ground floor, a small chamber with brocade curtains. Even today, I remember every tiny detail of it.

We sat down on a sofa that was covered with azure silk. For a little while, we did nothing more than look at one another without saying anything, just like the night before.

"I have spent years imagining this moment, Irene," the woman suddenly said, looking down. "And now that it has arrived, everything seems so strange that . . ." Her voice suddenly broke, and I noticed that her eyes had become shiny.

Instinctively, I reached over and clasped her hand. Then I bent down a bit to meet her eyes.

"Please tell me, ma'am. I beg you."

"Of course, Irene. Of course . . ." she said as the tears began to line her cheeks. Then she breathed a very heavy sigh, seeming to gather all her strength. She looked me in the eyes, and at last she spoke. "My name, Irene, is Alexandra Sophie von Klemnitz and . . . I am your mother."

★ ★ ★

I don't remember much else about that day. I recall that after several hours, my father finally arrived, straight from Amiens, where he had been for business. When he got out of the carriage in the duke's gardens, I went to meet him, forcing myself not to run.

Papa gave me a firm, serious look with his clear eyes, and then he hugged me as strongly as I had ever remembered him having done. We did not exchange a word.

In the garden behind me, my mother, Alexandra Sophie, watched us from the foot of the stone staircase of the mansion. The fountain there next to her murmured in its low, soft voice.

At dusk, a carriage took me to the *Boulevard de Courcelles*, where I had an appointment with Lupin and Sherlock — the latter of whom would be departing for London shortly. And as important as that goodbye was to me — a goodbye I knew was the prelude to months of longing — it was overshadowed by the words I'd heard that afternoon from the kind lips of that woman . . . my mother.

After we said farewell to Sherlock, and his carriage drew away along the roads of a semideserted Paris, it was Lupin's and my turn to say goodbye. It was understood that I would return that evening to Evreux with my father, while he would remain in Paris with his father.

We took a few steps toward the nearby *Parc Monceau*, where we stopped. Lupin leaned his back against the railing and stayed silent like that for a little while. The dusk light filtered through the linden branches. Their golden color promised warmer, gentler days and the arrival of spring.

Lupin and I looked into one another's eyes, and I noticed that his dark eyes had never seemed as big as they did at that moment.

"This adventure has finally come to an end," he said after a brief silence. "And this time, perhaps, we ventured farther than we'd expected."

Later on, I often asked myself what Arsène had meant, but right then, I only had one thought. Yes, this time our investigation had brought truly unexpected, unsettling news into my life.

"Goodbye, Irene." Lupin took my hand and gently pressed it to his. It was warm and dry, and it gave me a feeling of security, even though I always felt most myself when living through dangerous situations with him and Sherlock.

"Arsène . . ." I began, lowering my gaze.

"Yes?" he replied, with a smile. I could not tell if it was bold or embarrassed.

I looked him straight in the face, with my best smile. "Goodbye, Arsène."

And for that moment in time, that was all that could be said.

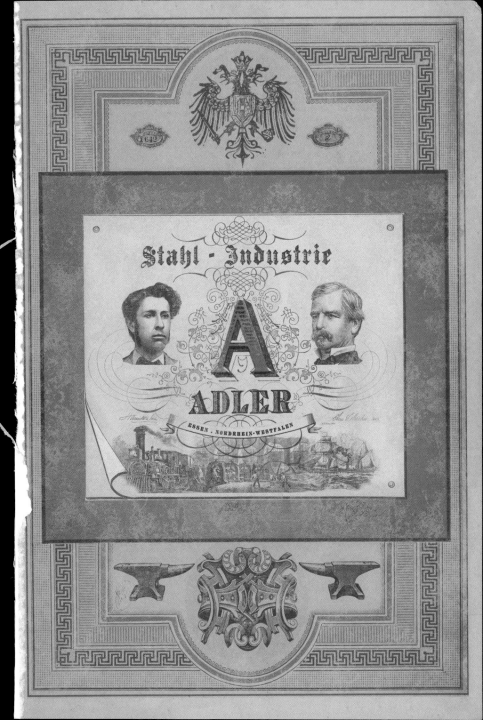

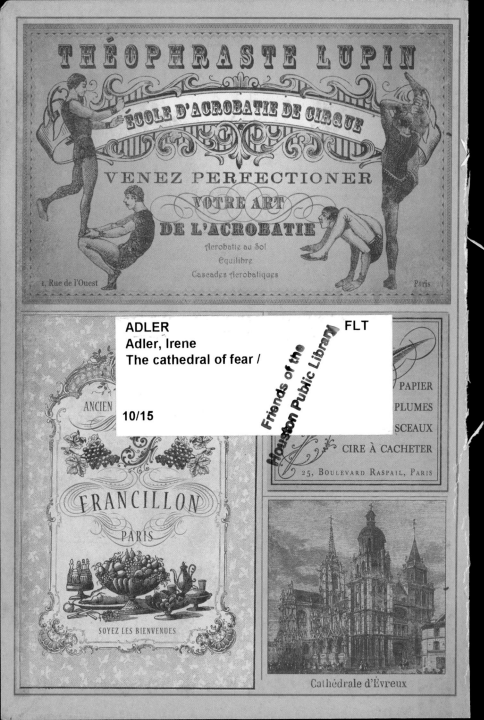